# The
# Breath
# of
# Darkness

a novel

## DARYLL SIMCOX

Jan-Carol
Publishing, Inc

*"every story needs a book"*

The Breath of Darkness
Daryll Simcox
Published June 2024
Little Creek Books
Imprint of Jan-Carol Publishing, Inc.
All rights reserved
Copyright © 2024 Daryll Simcox
Graphic Design: Tara Sizemore
Front Cover Photo: © Michael/Adobe Stock

ISBN: 978-1-962561-30-3
Library of Congress Control Number: 2024940263

You may contact the publisher:
Jan-Carol Publishing, Inc.
PO Box 701
Johnson City, TN 37605
publisher@jancarolpublishing.com
www.jancarolpublishing.com

I would like to thank you, the reader, for taking the time to enjoy my book. I hope that it will be as much fun for you to read as it was for me to write. Creating the characters and events of a book is something I have always dreamed of doing. Finally, with the help of my wife, I found the courage to put a story on paper, and once the process started I found myself totally engulfed in the book. The characters and the happenings at the port seemed to come to life. It was as though I was watching everything unfold before my eyes. I hope that you find yourself wanting to turn the page to see what happens next, and thanks again for reading THE BREATH OF DARKNESS.

# PROLOGUE

As the morning light began to appear on the small port and its surroundings, there was a calm that seemed to settle upon all that was visible. There were small wisps of fog that danced across the water and its gentle ripples with the help of the breeze. The small birds had begun to sing their songs, a bear and her cubs were walking along the shoreline looking for an easy morning meal, and the flowers that had only bloomed the week before were swaying back and forth with the breeze. The trees, the mountains, the bay, and all that was in view seemed like the perfect wilderness paradise.

It had been over seventy-five years since anyone had inhabited the port. Once a small thriving fishing community, it now lay abandoned, only home to what nature had intended to live and thrive in the area. There were still remnants scattered around that were left behind when the people left. The machinery, part of the processing facility, the workers homes, and various tools could be seen, but only barely. Nature had reclaimed her hold on the bay and its surroundings.

Why the people left so abruptly was an issue not often discussed. Some said they just simply did not adjust to living and working in this remote, isolated area. Some said the weather played a factor, especially in the winter months. The people of Port Chatham fishing village had a much different explanation for their departure. Some kept small journals which described the events that took place. Others gave eyewitness accounts, but nobody took them very seriously at the time. Nowadays, about the only people who even talked of Port Chatham were a small band of paranormal investigators, and among them, none had ever visited the area.

# CHAPTER 1

It had taken Rob Hutchins months to convince the network that his new reality show would be a hit and make them lots of money — the money being the final selling point for the executives at the office. There would be eight contestants, all vying for the big payout. The fewer contestants that remained at the end of one month, the larger the payday for each individual. In addition to the contestants, there would be two camera operators and two technicians. Two cabins were constructed for housing, and the supplies would be furnished.

The contestants would be informed of the history of the port. All individuals would arrive by boat, which is the only access to this area to this day. It all seemed like a great TV show in the making, but nobody knew exactly what would play out in the end.

All eight contestants were chosen by the network, which had made Rob's job much easier. He hired the two cameramen, Bill Sielt and Mark Wilson. He had known both of them for years — Mark since elementary school and Bill since college. Both of these men knew good technicians that they trusted to work on their personal equipment, which they insisted on using for the filming of the show. Rob assured Bill and Mark that the network would furnish top notch cameras and agreed to let them carry along their personal video equipment. Rob informed Mark and Bill that they would be carrying weapons for the protection of the others just in case they encountered any wild animals.

"However," Rob said, "we are going to add a little excitement to the adventure for the contestants."

"In what way?" Bill asked and glanced over to Rob.

Rob answered, "I have hired an expert outdoorsman, Bob Long, who we'll drop off a little further down the shoreline the day after you guys arrive. The main party arrives on Monday, and we'll drop him off Tuesday about noon. He'll then make his way up to an old hunting stand that was remodeled when the cabins were built."

Mark said, "So I'm assuming that Mr. Bob is supposed to bring the Port Chatham folklore to life for the other eight."

"Exactly," Rob said and smiled. "We want to put the fear into these people, but I want you and your technicians to show a little fear also. The more realistic the situation seems, the better it will appear on the ole TV tube, plus we don't want the others to realize that what's happening is not real. Mr. Long will be carrying a locator device which you and the techs can track with this monitor. Make sure on Tuesday that you can see him shortly after his arrival time. Any problems, call me on the SAT Phone."

"Any more surprises we need to know about?" Bill asked.

"Each of the contestants will have their own Go-Pro cameras to document any findings they may come across. The technicians may have to assist from time to time with the cameras," Rob answered.

"What exactly is the end goal for this game these people are playing?" Bill asked.

"All eight have been instructed to find any evidence of paranormal activity in the area," Rob replied. "There's a lot of history tied to the port and the people that inhabited it. The people of Port Chatham all left in a real big hurry, and some of them kept journals explaining the events that took place while they lived and worked there. There were eyewitness reports from others about what they called the 'Hairy Man.' Supposedly, the creature was what drove them all to leave."

"So, these contestants are trying to find out if this legend is real?" Mark asked.

"Yes," Rob said. "They all get paid an equal amount to do so. However, there are bonuses involved if they actually uncover any evidence, and each person's payout becomes larger for each one who decides to take an early exit. All in the spirit of a TV reality show so fans can tune into each week to watch."

"Do we split up to film their progress when they take their little scouting trips, or what?" Bill asked.

"No, I don't think that will be necessary since they have their Go-Pro cameras," Rob answered. "You can from time to time just so they can be filmed as a group."

"Will they just do their own filming during the night?" Bill asked. "I'm guessing that's when Bob will be working his magic."

"They probably will film when things start going bump in the night," Rob replied. "But just in case they don't, we installed remote cameras in the cabins. That way we can monitor the contestants while they are alone and confer with you guys if we need to. Remember, Bob is out there alone, and if he needs any assistance, he will contact you. And for goodness sakes, make sure neither one of you shoots Bob. Not only would that possibly be bad for Bob, but if you miss, he might shoot back, and he is an expert after all." Rob winked.

"Bob's food has been added to your supplies," Rob added. "He eats very light, and his supplies are labeled. Someone will need to set it out each night so he can grab it before he goes back to the stand. It's labeled by name and numerically for each night's pickup. There is a box on your cabin deck to place it in."

# CHAPTER 2

The following week, on Monday, May 8, all of the contestants and crew assembled at the parting dock for the beginning of the big adventure. The crew's equipment had already been loaded, and the contestants' bags were swiftly carried on by the ship's deckhands. Bill and Mark were busy filming small clips of all the happenings for the show's beginning. The technicians, Andre and Tim, were down below checking out some of the equipment.

None of the contestants had ever met each other or any of the crew. As the boat slowly began to leave the port, everyone introduced themselves.

First up were the cameramen. Bill, a medium-build man with blond hair went first.

"Hello, everyone, I'm Bill Sielt. I'm forty-two years old and from California."

Mark was next to chime in. "My name is Mark Wilson, and I'm a little younger than Bill. I'm sure all of you could tell that, though."

After everyone finished laughing, Rob interrupted, "There are two technicians below deck checking out equipment. They will help with any difficulties while at the port, including the cameras provided to you."

The first contestant introduced himself.

"My name is Dave Murrows, forty-four years old, and from Ohio."

The second contestant followed. "Hi. I'm Shelley Winslow, from

Louisiana, and I'm a very young thirty-six years old."

Everyone fell in love with Shelley's Cajun accent.

The third contestant introduced herself by raising her hand. "Sasha Holdings from California, Asian American, and I'm thirty-two."

The fourth contestant tilted his camouflage cap and said, "Willie Cantrell from Nashville, Tennessee."

The next contestant was the youngest competitor and was sporting a cowboy hat. "I'm Stan Bunter from Texas, and I'm just a baby at only twenty years old."

Everybody on the top deck chuckled.

The next contestant smiled and said, "My name is Betty Davidson from Michigan. Not going to tell you people my age, but my babies are twenty-eight and twenty-five."

Once again, everyone laughed.

The seventh contestant introduced himself. "I'm Ronnie Blount, originally from North Carolina, but now I reside in Arizona."

Everyone was waiting and looked at the eighth contestant. They were sure she had to be some Olympic athlete or professional track star.

She smiled and said, "Sandy Everly, thirty-eight, and I am into real estate."

Everybody looked at Sandy with amazement because she looked like an athlete of some kind. She was medium in height, very well-toned, and looked like she could run any distance with ease.

Willy was first to speak up about her appearance. "First off, there is no way you are thirty-eight years old. And I'm not sure about the rest of these people, but I had you figured for somebody who won a few gold medals or track championships of some kind."

Sandy just smiled and said, "I am that old, but I guess I was just blessed with this body. I did some running in high school and college, but now I only run from house to house to make a living."

***

As the ship cleared the port, Rob briefed everyone on the rules and regulations of the game. Everyone had a copy and studied the rules and regulations, and all were well aware of the history of their destination.

Rob looked at the contestants and restated, "Once again, I just want to make sure that all of you fully understand the material given to you and that there are no questions."

All nodded affirmatively.

Rob added, "Everybody signed the appropriate paperwork to clear anyone of responsibility for what happens while at the port?"

Once again, all nodded affirmatively.

As he surveyed the group, Rob asked, "Anyone ready to back out?"

They all chuckled, resembling a bunch of teenagers getting ready to board a rollercoaster.

"The camera guys and technicians have the radios to call for help or early departure. Also, we had to add another person to the crew, Dr. Elaine Lotle. This was per the network's request just because we can only reach the port by boat and not necessarily in a moment's notice."

Rob knew that if they had to get there quickly, they could take a plane and land on the water. But it made for better drama if the contestants thought otherwise.

The doctor and the medical supplies for minor situations were a late decision made by the network to cover their rear end. Rob didn't really mind, and it just meant a few more supplies had to be carried ashore.

As if on cue, the door coming onto the deck opened, and Dr. Lotle gracefully appeared. She was a young, tall blonde who, ninety percent of the time, wore her hair in a ponytail. She was not much of an outdoor person, but what the network was willing to pay her would go a long way in clearing her student loans.

"Ladies and gentlemen, Dr. Elaine Lotle," Rob stated as he pointed toward her.

Everyone looked at Elaine.

For a moment, it caught her off guard, and then she grinned. "Nice to meet all of you. We ready to do this, people?"

The group all acknowledged her by giving her smiles and a thumbs up.

*** 

The boat ride to the port was a pleasant one with no rough water, and the sun was shining bright. There was plenty for the contestants to talk about as they mingled on the deck. They discussed the scenery, the port, and its history. Each of them had their own ideas about why the people left the fishing village so abruptly, but most agreed that they were not sure about this Hairy Man theory. All of the contestants expressed this uncertainty except for Shelley and Ronnie.

Ronnie approached Shelley and said, "I noticed when everyone was talking, you had some doubt about this Hairy Man theory."

"I have never seen anything like that, but my cousin swears he did once," Shelley responded.

"Where? In Louisiana?" Ronnie asked.

"Yes. He was an avid hunter and fisherman, but he no longer goes into the woods. At first, his buddies would make fun of him. He said that it kinda bothered him for a while, but he decided he didn't care...He knew what he saw, and he didn't want to see it again."

Ronnie interjected, "Like I told everyone, I grew up in North Carolina. When I was a young boy, about twelve, my buddies and I were walking in the mountains behind our homes. We lived in a small black community at the base of the mountains, and one day, we saw something. I really don't know what we even saw that day. I do know that we came across a dead animal...a deer...but we could smell something that wasn't the deer. Then we heard footsteps in the woods above us. There was a low, almost grunting, growling sound. Well, you know what twelve-year-old minds can do, so we took off running. Every time we would stop, we could hear something above us. One of my friends, Jeremy, said that he saw a tall, hairy figure peeking around a tree at us...but I didn't see it. I just know it put the fear in me for a long time. I wouldn't go out after dark, and I definitely stayed away from the mountains."

"Did you tell anyone?" asked Shelley.

"That night at supper, with a little hesitation, I told my mother and father about what happened. I was kinda expecting for them to make fun of me, but instead my mom looked at my dad and said, 'It's back again.' I quickly asked what was back, and all she said was for me to stay out of the mountains. She made me promise to not go up there anymore. As I got older, I asked them about the mountains, but all they ever say was that there was a mean, old man who lived up there," Ronnie answered.

"What do you think it was?" asked Shelley.

Ronnie replied, "I don't know, but I don't believe it was just an angry old man. That deer hadn't been shot or anything, and it looked like its neck had been broken and torn from its body. I never believed a man could do that to a deer, no matter how angry or mean he was."

"Maybe we will both get some answers up here," Shelley said.

"Maybe," Ronnie replied.

\*\*\*

Rob, the cameramen, the techs, and Elaine sat together in a small cabin inside the ship. Rob interjected in the conversation, "Since Dr. Elaine was brought in on such a short notice, we need to brief her on all the activities for the group."

"First off, I want everyone to simply address me as Elaine," she said. "I'm just glad I got this opportunity to go on this adventure and to participate."

Rob said with a smile, "It's funny you called it an adventure, because for the eight people out there on the deck, that is exactly what they are going to get."

"How so?" asked Elaine.

Rob explained to Dr. Elaine about Bob Long, the remote cameras, and the firearms that Mark and Bill were carrying.

After he finished, Elaine said, "I was going to ask if anyone was carrying any weapons for protection. So, basically, my job is to treat any small injuries that occur and assess medical situations. And...to watch these eight people come apart at the seams with fear."

The other five laughed and Bill said, "This should be quite interesting, to say the least. Plus, we get a free camping trip to enjoy the great outdoors."

"By the way, Dr. Elaine—" Rob started but was interrupted.

"No 'Doctor' — just Elaine," she said.

Rob continued, "I already forgot. Make sure you go along with these guys and show a little fear yourself, Elaine. We want this to be as realistic as possible."

Elaine raised her wine glass and said, "Will do, boss."

They all laughed again as they raised their glasses to toast her.

***

After what seemed like forever, the boat steered around a long point stacked with enormous protruding rocks and began to enter the bay. Everyone was on the deck of the boat enjoying the majestic view. The bay was beautiful, the sun was glistening on the water, the birds were soaring effortlessly above the bay, and a gentle breeze was causing the leaves on the trees to dance with one another. All seemed well and perfect.

They slowly passed by the last standing section of the processing plant. It came into view as the boat slowed and then came to a complete halt, even with the old landing dock.

The captain assembled everyone together on the boat. He gave strict instructions for boarding the craft that would take them ashore.

"Okay, people. This is your last chance to reconsider. Anyone want to go back with us on this beautiful, safe boat?" Rob asked.

Some of the contestants said out loud, "No," while the others just nodded their heads negative.

The transition from the boat to the raft went well for all of them, even though it had to be repeated several times to get everybody and everything ashore. As the raft departed for the last time, everyone gave a hearty wave to Rob and the boat crew.

On the face of the captain, however, there was a slight hint of concern.

Rob asked, "Captain, why the strange look?"

"I'm not sure about this, Rob," the captain said. "The stories about this place give me a funny feeling."

Rob chuckled. "Don't tell me you believe in this so-called Hairy Man?"

"I've lived in this region a long time, and I have heard all the stories, even when I was a young man," the captain replied. "There's a reason this place is still uninhabited to this day. I've never seen this Hairy Man, but something lives here. And I think it's evil."

Everybody grabbed their gear, and they heard the boat start up. Some turned to look as it pulled away.

Stan said, "Well, I reckon I'm not in Texas anymore."

"I'd say. It looks like no other place I've seen," Betty said. "But you have to admit, the view is fantastic."

Dave Murrows, a tall, lanky man, grabbed his duffel bag and said, "I guess all that's left now is to get up this hill, settle into our new facilities, and wait on this Hairy Guy."

Everyone agreed. They started toward the cabins. The shoreline was covered with rocks; however, there was just enough sandy soil for one to walk comfortably. There was a trail winding up the bank through the brush that the cabin construction crew had obviously made when they were here.

"This looks like the path to our new home," Betty said.

"Everybody good at carrying their own gear?" Willy said. "This trail may be a little slippery."

Everyone glanced up at Willy with looks on their faces that said, "I can take care of myself."

"I wouldn't want anyone to strain themselves and have to make an early exit," Willy added.

They all laughed with just a hint of sarcasm and began moving up the trail. They reached the cabins and lugged their gear up the steps onto the deck. They all turned just in time to see the boat exiting the bay.

# CHAPTER 3

Stan opened the door for the contestants' cabin, and one by one they entered.

Sandy said, "Oh, this is a lot nicer than I imagined it would be. Not exactly roughing it in the great outdoors."

Willy quickly added, "Not exactly a chalet in the Great Smoky Mountains, but almost. If it had a hot tub, it would be pretty close."

Everyone laughed, especially when his pronunciation of the word "pretty" sounded more like "purty."

"Glad someone else says purty. Didn't want all you people laughing at just me," Stan said.

There were two bedrooms with four bunks — one bedroom for the guys and one for the gals. The cabin had a spacious sitting room with a rock fireplace and a kitchen with all the amenities. There was a generator that supplied power for the stove, lights, and the well pump along with a small water heater for taking showers.

The contestants decided which bedroom was for them and deposited their gear appropriately. All claimed a bunk and placed their sleeping bags on them.

The camera guys, techs, and Dr. Elaine had a cabin that was much the same, except there was only one bedroom that all five would share.

"Elaine, they built our cabin a little smaller," Mark said. "Only one bed-room for four guys. They weren't planning for a fifth person, especially a woman, to accompany us."

"That's perfectly fine by me," Elaine responded. "I'm not sure I want to be in a room by myself out here. I like the idea that four guys will be looking out for my well-being on this camping trip."

"At least they threw in another bunk so all of us guys didn't have to draw straws to see who was going to sleep on the floor," Andre said.

Elaine said, "I'm glad that you said 'guys' and didn't include me in draw-ing straws."

"We got to make sure your stay is comfortable," Bill said and grinned. "Never know when you might have to give one of us medical attention... can't have you upset with us."

"That's right, keep the ole doc on your good side," Elaine said, grinning back.

Tim started the generator, and the lights came on in the cabins. Even though nobody else showed a noticeable reaction, Sasha was quick to give a thumbs up, but the others felt a small sigh of relief.

In just a few minutes, Willy and Dave had the fires going in both of the cabins. Even though the temperature was fairly mild, there was a dampness in the air. This area was known to get a lot of precipitation throughout the year. The fires would make for a much more comfortable environment even during the daylight hours.

After all had settled into their cabins, they mingled on the decks for a little while. The cabins were right next to each other, so communicating as a group was effortless. Most of the conversations consisted of just small talk, but already it seemed like the group had meshed together well. They decided that they would all eat together each night in the contestants' cabin. This would help in the filming of the group. About an hour before dark, the crew walked over to the other cabin so they could begin supper.

All eight contestants were on the deck looking out across the bay.

Tech Tim was the first to speak to the group.

"Is everybody ready to start supper?" he asked. "I'm starved."

They all began to laugh.

Betty commented, "We were just debating on who was going to walk over and get you guys."

"Looked like, to me, you were enjoying the view," Tim said.

"We didn't want to look too obvious, but we concluded that if you didn't come soon, we were going to start cooking without you," Sandy added.

Everybody laughed.

Bill said, "Well, let's get this party started."

They all went inside and decided, after looking through the pantry, that tonight's menu would involve beans.

Stan raised his hands and said, "I'm not the greatest cook in the world, but I can make a mean dish of cowboy beans."

Even though some of them were not exactly sure what cowboy beans consisted of and they had some doubt, they all agreed to give it a try.

The cooler on the boat had been more than sufficient to keep all the meat cool on their way to the port. The generator would keep their supplies good for the entire month. Stan removed a package of hamburger and began to fry it on the stove.

"Anything I can do to help?" Shelley asked.

"We'll need bowls and spoons for everyone, and we can put these cans of beans in the pot to warm," Stan replied.

Shelley smiled and said, "Okay, master chef."

"By the look on everyone's face, I don't think they are very sure about these cowboy beans," Stan chuckled.

"Once they start eating them, I believe you will have their approval," Shelley said, and smiled again.

After the hamburger was finished cooking, Stan added the beans and let them simmer for a while. He found some seasoning in the cabinet, and in a little while, he had a meal fit for the finest wagon train around.

All thirteen people sat around the cabin — some at the table, some in the sitting area, and two of the women sat at the hearth of the fireplace. The fire was crackling as they enjoyed their bowl of beans.

"Stan, these beans are really good," Sandy said. "You are going to have to give me the recipe."

"They're really easy," Stan replied. "When you're young and single, this is the way to cook."

After they finished eating and the dishes were cleaned, they all decided to sit around the outdoor firepit and wind down a little from an exhausting day. Once again, Willy and Dave performed their fire-making magic, and within minutes there was a roaring fire. Bill and Mark filmed as the others began to speak.

Stan started the conversation and spoke first. "So, what do y'all think really happened here over seventy-five years ago?" he asked.

"I'm not really sure. Maybe it was a bear that was responsible," Ronnie said.

"Did everyone research the events that took place here?" Shelley asked.

Everyone verbally answered, "Yes," or nodded affirmatively and looked around at each other.

"I'm not sure either," Willy said. "I'm no paranormal expert by no means, but whatever happened was done by something physical...something that was real and brutal."

"The descriptions in the journals were of a tall figure covered with hair," Betty said. "The people simply called it the Hairy Man. Some even drew crude pictures of it."

"Like a Yeti or Sasquatch?" Sasha asked.

"There are different names for a creature like this all over the world," Sandy replied. "There's even pictures and video. However, most are not clear enough to definitively show what one is looking at."

"This is true, but I've experienced things back home while hunting or hiking in the woods that I could not explain," Dave said. "Once, while hunting, I saw something. Now, it was a way off and moving through a laurel patch...but I never witnessed anything like it."

"What did it look like?" Ronnie asked.

"It was tall and dark..." Dave paused looked down and then looked back up. He continued, "I can't say for sure, but it looked like it was covered with hair, and it was walking upright like a man. I only got to see it for maybe fifteen seconds, since it only walked between the laurel bushes. I just don't know."

"Down home, there's always talk about a creature like this," Shelley said with wide eyes. "Heck, even my cousin claims to have seen one. Maybe he did, or maybe he didn't. But I do know that he will not go into the woods anymore, and he was an avid hunter."

"My buddies and I ran into something back where I grew up," Ronnie said, looking at each contestant. "It was a small community in North Carolina. We were exploring up in the mountains behind our homes one afternoon when we came upon a dead deer. It had not been shot. It was like its head had been torn from its body. The head was still lying there next to the body. I had never seen anything like that before. Then, we heard this growling sound. Our young minds were running with fear, and soon our bodies were outrunning our minds as we raced down the mountain. Every time we stopped to catch our breath, we heard something coming behind us. It seemed to be driving us out of the woods instead of trying to catch us."

"Did you ever get a glimpse of it?" Stan asked.

"I didn't. But my buddy, Jeremy, said that he seen it staring at us when we stopped one time. He described it much the same way as Dave did. All I know...my heart was pounding out of my chest by the time I got home."

"Did you tell anyone?" Betty asked.

"I told my mother and father that night at supper," Ronnie replied.

"What did they say?" Stan asked.

"My mom looked up at my dad and said, 'It's back again.' She then proceeded to tell me not to go up in the mountains again and made me promise, which I did without any hesitation. As I got older, I would ask them from time to time about what was in the mountains. All they ever said was that there was a mean, old man that lived up there. But that day, what we encountered was no man."

Andre and Tim looked at each other. Both grinned and turned their heads away from Ronnie. Andre thought to himself, *This is shaping up nicely. Maybe Rob was right about this reality show after all.*

Elaine did not speak up. She just sat there quietly enjoying the fire and the beautiful night. She could not help but wonder about these stories, though, since she had never witnessed anything like this. It appeared that all the contestants did not have any definitive answers about what they had heard or seen. So, Elaine did wonder, could there be some truth to this?

The group continued to talk, but the conversation slowly moved to talking about each individual's interests and their families. Some talked about hunting, some fishing, and even sports made its way into the first night's conversation among the contestants. As the fire began to dwindle down, they carried their wine glasses back into the cabin.

It was about nine-thirty when everyone decided to call it a night. The crew said their goodnights to the contestants and walked to their cabin. The cabins were not separated by more than thirty feet and just a little farther between each cabin's steps, which were located in the center of the decks. The crew walked by with flashlights as they started up the steps. That's when Mark noticed that Andre was standing, almost frozen, about halfway between the cabins.

"What's the matter, Andre?" Mark asked.

"Did you guys hear that?" Andre asked.

"Hear what?" Bill asked.

"Down the shoreline, a low grunting sound," Andre answered.

"Don't tell me you're getting spooked now," Tim said. "It's supposed to be the poor people over there that get the scare of a lifetime."

"I didn't say I was spooked...not yet anyway," Andre said.

They all laughed. However, they stood on the deck for a little while just to see if they could maybe hear it again. But there were no more noises to be heard, other than the normal nightly creatures of the bay.

Everyone in both cabins settled in for the night.

In the contestants' cabin, Sasha said, "I know we have separate rooms for the men and women, but I think I would feel a little safer if we had a mixed group in each room."

Betty, Sandy, and Shelley all laughed.

Sasha looked at them and said, "Okay, I'll admit the campfire stories kind of got to me a little."

"I don't think that's why we are laughing. I know I feel the same way as you," Sandy said.

"Well, the rooms are pretty spacious. Why don't we just move all the bunks into one room and put our gear in the other?" Stan suggested.

"Do the rest of you guys mind?" Sandy asked.

They all agreed, and the guys began to move the bunks all into one room. From the crew's cabin, Tim looked out the window and began to laugh out loud.

Andre raised up from adjusting his sleeping bag and asked, "What's so funny?"

"Apparently, you're not the only one who got a little spooked by the campfire stories," Tim answered.

"What do you mean?" Andre asked.

"Looks like the contestants have all decided to occupy the same room for sleeping tonight," Tim said.

Elaine looked out the window and said, "Can't say that I blame them. There's safety in numbers, guys."

Everyone settled into their bunks, and all had a very restful night. There were no surprises during the darkness. At least none that anyone was aware of...yet.

# CHAPTER 4

Bill was the first to rise in the crew's cabin the next morning. He quickly started a pot of coffee for the rest of them. He had just poured himself a mug and was standing at the front window looking out over the bay when Tim walked inside. The bay looked like a painting one would see in an art gallery. Tim grabbed a cup, poured his coffee, and strolled over to the fireplace. He placed another log on the fire even though it was not necessary. It was as though he had something on his mind.

Tim looked at Bill, glanced around the room to make sure they were alone, and said, "I know that I made fun of Andre last night, but I also heard that sound down the shoreline. I didn't want to scare Elaine, because it didn't appear that she heard anything, but I'm going to apologize to Andre."

"I don't think he took what you said to heart," Bill said. "And by the way, I heard something too. Maybe it was a bear...I don't know, but it was different than anything I've ever heard before."

The conversation ended as the others awoke and filtered into the room. The others got themselves a cup of encouragement for the morning, and all made small talk among the crew as they drank their coffee.

After finishing their coffee and putting on their attire for the day, the crew ambled over to the contestants' cabin to have breakfast. As they approached the steps, Betty opened the door and said, "You people ready for some breakfast?"

The crew all nodded yes and began walking up the steps. Most of them were going through the door or walking across the deck when Andre noticed something strange. There was a perfectly round stone sitting on the banister railing to the left of the steps. It was about the size of a large marble. He knew it wasn't there last night when they left to go to their cabin. He knew that because he was at the back of the crew parade and didn't have his flashlight. He remembered sliding his hand along the railing to be sure of his footing. If the stone had been there, he would have surely bumped it with his hand. That wasn't there last night. *I'm sure of it*, he thought.

As the crew entered the cabin, they were greeted with the smell of bacon, eggs, and toast. Apparently, the contestants had gotten up early as well, and they all had lent a hand in making the morning meal. This was a welcome gesture to the crew.

"Thank you, guys, for getting breakfast ready. We appreciate it," Bill said.

"You're welcome," Sasha said. "I heard an awful noise just before daylight that woke me up, and I could not go back to sleep."

Andre looked up at Sasha. "I thought a bear had gotten into the cabin during the night, but then I realized that it was just one of these guys snoring," Sasha said and snickered.

"It could have been me," Willy said, grinning. "My family calls me the old sleeping bear. If I go to sleep watching TV, they usually have to turn up the volume."

Everyone sat around the cabin eating their food and drinking their coffee. There wasn't much chit-chat this morning. There were no set plans or rules to follow for the show, but they all knew that extra money was involved if they could prove that there was something strange that happened here so many years ago. This was motivation for all to snoop around a little.

After last night's conversation around the firepit, curiosity was starting to nip at the contestants. They pretty much had the run of the day to do whatever they desired. The supplies were set up for everyone to eat breakfast and dinner, but lunch was on each individual. This way, if they discovered anything during the day or something occurred at night, Mark and Bill could catch the events on film as they talked about them.

Everybody finished the morning breakfast, and all pitched in to clean up the mess. The crew started back over to the cabin when Bill informed the contestants, "We are going to recharge our equipment and check on a few things. Maybe around midday we will do some filming as a group. In the meantime, make sure everyone carries their GoPro cameras to document anything you might find."

Just as they got to the door, Elaine said, "Remember, if anyone gets as much as a scratch, I want you to come and see me. We don't want a major infection to set up. And besides, I do not want to look bad for the TV show. That would not be good for my professional career."

All the contestants laughed and promised Elaine they would come and see her immediately if they got injured, no matter how small it was.

At the crew's cabin, they did a quick equipment check and put everything on charge. Tim asked, "What time is it? I want to check out the locator monitor when ole Bob the outdoorsman arrives."

"His arrival time should be in about another half hour. Hope he doesn't get delayed. Looks like there might be some weather coming in," Bill answered.

Fortunately, just like clockwork, Rob and the boat crew were able to drop Bob off with five minutes to spare before noon. After gathering up his gear, Bob disappeared into the woods to begin his trek to his remodeled hunting stand.

As the boat had once again cleared the bay, the SAT Phone on the table in the crew cabin rang.

Tim answered the phone and said, "Hello?"

"Is this Tim?" Rob asked.

"Yes, it is. Bill and Mark are checking cameras. Andre is getting the locator monitor ready."

"Great," Rob said. "We dropped Bob off about ten minutes ago. I'd like to make sure you can see him on the monitor. I want the crew to know where he is at all times and to make sure he's okay."

Tim called the others and said, "Hey, guys. Bob has landed. Let's see if we can get him on the monitor."

Andre hit the power button. "Monitor on and there he is. I'd say that he's approximately five miles west of us and appears to be making his way north."

"Sounds good," Rob responded. "I'll let him know that you guys have him on the monitor. Please check in on him periodically since he's alone. He should have a small hike north, and then he'll trek east to intercept your position."

"Roger that," Tim acknowledged.

"Out for now," Rob said, and the line went dead.

Tim looked at the others. "I guess it would have been too much trouble for him to have let me say goodbye."

Bill and Mark smiled, and Andre just shook his head in disbelief.

Bob Long's trek wasn't going to be that bad, even though his gear was quite heavy. The climbs were going to be a little challenging, but he would manage. The game trails in the area provided excellent pathways to get to his first destination, which would be his new home for a few weeks. He was quite happy when he arrived at the newly remodeled hunting stand. It was well insulated, and it would be no problem for him to stay warm and dry. He could not have a wood fire, because he didn't want to give anything away to the contestants. He could cook the food the crew provided on a small camp stove.

The weather deteriorated just as he was getting settled in. The clouds lowered down on the surrounding mountains, the breeze picked up, and it began to drizzle. Bob smirked and thought to himself, *Perfect night for a little mischief in the woods.*

Back at the cabins, Mark and Bill stood on the deck, filming the group. They had ventured down the path to the bay and were investigating the old fish processing facility. They were curiously looking along the shore, and some even took the opportunity to climb up on what was left of the facility and walk on its walkway.

Elaine walked up and said, "Oh, great. We're probably fixing to have our first recordable injury."

Mark stopped filming, looked at Elaine, and said, "Would not surprise me at all."

Elaine looked across the bay. "Here comes the rain. Wonder how fast they can run back up that path to the cabin? I'll bet Sandy beats them all."

"Would not surprise me at all. I believe Sandy does a little more exercising than just running from house to house to make a sale," Tim said.

They were correct. By the time the group reached the path, Sandy was out front and pulling away from the others. Nobody paid much attention to the surroundings as they raced to outrun the rain, but Sasha and Sandy noticed a distinctive odor in a particular part of the trail. As they reached the cabin deck, thrilled they had beaten the rain, one by one they darted through the cabin door that Sandy had graciously opened since she had finished first in getting to the cabin.

Sasha stopped at the door and glanced back down the path.

Sandy stood just inside the doorway as Sasha stopped before entering and turned to look back. "Enjoying the view, or did you notice something?" Sandy asked.

"There was a strange odor. I smelled it coming up the path," Sasha answered.

"What did it smell like to you?" asked Sandy.

"So, you noticed it too?" Sasha asked.

Sandy stared into Sasha's eyes. "Yes. It was a kinda wet, musky smell... not very pleasant."

Sasha returned the stare. "Musky a little, but almost like the scent of a dead animal."

"Sorry, but you being from California, I wouldn't have thought you'd encountered that many dead animals," Sandy said.

Sasha grinned and said, "I do a lot of hiking in the mountains...almost every weekend. It's pretty normal to come across a dead animal carcass every now and then."

Sandy was surprised. "Really?" she asked.

"Oh, yes, there are quite a few cougars where we hike. You have to be on guard at all times." But after taking one more glance down the trail, Sasha added, "I'm just not sure what it was."

Sasha, for some reason, had the strange feeling they were being watched as the contestants came up the trail. She had that same feeling at times when hiking back home. This time, it was different. She couldn't figure out why.

Later in the afternoon, the rain stopped. The clouds were persistent, but at least everyone could venture back outside. The contestants grabbed their cameras and decided to go back down to the processing facility. Sasha paid close attention as they descended down to the shoreline. Sandy did the same. This time, there were no strange odors that alarmed them. Still, Sasha had an uneasy feeling. She was unable to put her finger on it. She convinced herself that she was just being paranoid.

Once down at the facility, the eight scoured around, looking for any clues that might present themselves. Mark and Bill filmed the progress as they inched their way around. Unknowingly, they had drifted apart and had become two investigative groups. Even with more ground covered in this manner, there didn't seem to be any clues.

The group that had moved up the bay from the facility stopped when Stan suddenly raised his head, turned on a dime, and almost lost his cowboy hat. He looked up into the woods. With the hat tilted back on his head, Stan asked, "You guys hear that?"

"There's something up the hillside in the woods," Shelley answered quickly. "I can hear it moving."

Bill lowered the camera and thought to himself, *Great, I'm fixing to have to pull my gun and scare a bear off on our first full day. And then, I'll have to explain to the group why we are carrying weapons.*

The thought had just cleared Bill's head when, suddenly, the group heard something crashing down the hillside toward them. All stood frozen in their tracks. Bill's hand was still on the pistol. He could hear his heart pounding. About twenty feet in front of the group, a rock the size of a softball rolled out of the tree line, bounced on a couple of its sister rocks, and splashed into the edge of the bay. There was nothing but silence. No movement in the woods. Nothing crashing down the hill. You could hear only the ripples left in the water.

After a short pause, Stan broke the silence and said, "Probably just a deer that we spooked coming up the shoreline."

"Yeah, probably," Shelley offered. "It dislodged the rock when it started to run."

"Well, people," Ronnie began, changing the mood of the conversation, "it's going to be dark in a little while, and with the help of the rain, we have just about wasted our entire first day. I say we get back and fix some dinner. I'm starving."

The group agreed and headed back to meet the others. When they all joined up, Dave asked, "Find any clues?"

"No, but we did have a deer throw a rock at us," Shelley said seriously.

"That's odd," Betty remarked. "I've never seen a deer that could throw anything, especially a rock."

Shelley noticed that Betty was no longer looking her in the eye but was staring right past her, down to the shoreline. The others had already turned and were walking toward the path when Shelley asked Betty, "What's the matter, Betty?"

"I could have sworn something was moving at the tree line where your group was just at," Betty said. "It appeared to be a dark figure staring back at us, and it ducked back into the tree line. Oh, I don't know...Maybe it was the shadows or maybe this place is already starting to get to me. My mind is playing tricks on me."

Shelley and Betty turned and hurried to catch up to the others. They all climbed the path to the cabins. Betty could not get the image out of her mind. She kept thinking that there had to be an explanation for what she had just seen, but she just couldn't come up with one. As they cleared the waist high brush at the top of the pathway, Tim and Andre were there, leaning on the railing around the deck.

"We thought we were going to have to eat without you guys," Tim said.

"I told these people I was starving when we were on the shoreline," Ronnie said. "We're going to need a table for thirteen."

"Let Bill and me put these heavy cameras back in the cabin and get our smaller personal cameras," Mark said. "Grab Elaine, and we'll be right over."

As the cameramen entered their cabin, Elaine asked, "Did anyone find anything interesting?"

"Nothing really special. Bill's group had a rock thrown at them by a deer," Mark replied.

"I didn't know that it was possible for a deer to do that. It didn't hit anyone, I hope," Elaine said with skepticism.

"I'm not sure where that rock came from, but luckily there were no injuries," Bill said.

Bill, Mark, and Elaine walked into the contestants' cabin and were met with the smell of hamburgers cooking. They heard jovial sounds of the others talking about the day's adventures. Some of the contestants were giving their explanations of the incident with the rock, while others were laughing and making fun of them.

"Sorry, guys, we took a vote without you and decided that hamburgers were on the menu tonight," Ronnie said proudly.

Elaine rubbed her hands together and said, "Not a problem. Excellent choice."

The group of thirteen sat down and devoured their hamburgers and potato chips. There was a lot of small talk as they ate, but they were mostly concerned with fighting off the day's hunger.

Bill noticed that Betty wasn't conferring much with the group. She appeared to be in thought and a million miles away. He approached her as she stood next to the window and stared out into what was swiftly becoming darkness. He gently touched her elbow as he came up to her.

She jumped as though something had grabbed her, and she yelled.

"I'm sorry, Betty!" Bill said. "I didn't mean to startle you. Is everything okay?"

"Yeah, I reckon so," Betty answered. "Just can't seem to get something off my mind. I saw, um...Oh, I don't know what I saw."

"What are you talking about, Betty?" Bill asked.

"Down at the bay today, right after we all met up to come back up here, and I was talking to Shelley...I think I saw something down the shoreline. It sounds silly, but it was a very large, dark figure. It was standing in the tree line, staring at us. I'm not sure 'cause it disappeared back into the woods almost as soon as I saw it. So, maybe my mind was playing tricks on me."

Bill looked Betty in the eyes and said, "Maybe tomorrow some of us should walk back down there and take a look. There wouldn't be any harm in checking it out and seeing if we can find any evidence. That way, we would know for sure."

Betty lifted her head and looked Bill in the eyes and said, "I would appreciate that. Maybe it would help to clear it from my mind."

"Sounds like a plan. First thing in the morning, we'll check it out," Bill assured her.

Betty smiled and patted Bill on the shoulder.

Shortly after the meal, the crew said their goodnights and retreated to their cabin. It didn't take long for the eight contestants to settle in. All were hoping for a better day tomorrow.

# CHAPTER 5

Once back in their cabin, Elaine asked, "Bill, was something wrong with Betty tonight? I noticed she didn't have a lot to say. She was kind of just staring out the window."

"She thinks she saw something today down at the bay, and it kinda got her shook up," Bill replied. "I told her a few of us would check it out first thing in the morning."

Tim looked at them and asked, "What did she see?"

Bill turned, looked at Tim, and said, "She's not sure. She thinks it was a very large, dark figure standing just in the tree line, staring at all of us. It was right at the spot where the rock came rolling down the hill, but she said that it disappeared almost as quickly as she realized it was there. Andre, let's check the monitor and see where Bob is. You don't think he got an early start on his tactics, do ya?"

Andre picked up the monitor, turned it on, and said, "If he did, he came all the way over here and then went back to his place. It's showing him right at the location of his stand. The same place he was all afternoon during the rain."

Mark sat down. "Surely, he would not have walked all the way over here to make an appearance and then retreated. That doesn't make any sense."

"Alright, guys, now you're starting to make me feel a little uneasy," Elaine said.

"I wouldn't think much of it, but whatever it was, it really shook her up," Bill said. "She was in her own little world at dinner, and when I touched her elbow and said her name, she just about jumped out of her skin. She had a look of fear in her eyes when she looked at me."

"Okay, guys, first off, I want to apologize to Andre," Tim said. "When I made fun of you for hearing that sound last night on the trip back over here, that was wrong. I did it because Elaine said nothing about it, so basically, I didn't think she heard it. But the truth is, I heard it too. I've never heard any animal make a sound like that. It was, I don't know, different. Andre, I heard that grunting sound also. Bill and I were talking about it this morning when the rest of you came into the kitchen."

Tim smiled at the group.

"Well, I appreciate you people acting like I was crazy," Andre said and grinned.

"Were none of you going to include me on this little happening?" Elaine asked.

They all looked around at each other, and Bill said, "From now on, we should share all information. We are a team, and we need to look after each other."

All agreed and decided to call it a night. It was time to see what Bob had in store for the group.

As Bill was laying in his sleeping bag, he couldn't help but think about Betty and what she had seen.

*If she did see something, would Bob encounter it in the darkness?* Bill thought. *Maybe it was just her imagination, or maybe it was something real. Sure hope they can figure that out tomorrow when they investigate the spot.*

After a small amount of time, all had drifted to sleep.

\*\*\*

Back at the stand, Bob suddenly was awakened from his nap by the beeping sound from his watch alarm. He rubbed his eyes and tried to focus on the time. Ten-thirty. Time to get ready and hike over to the cabins.

He dressed in his camouflage outerwear that had been designed to match the elements of the bay area and ate a quick snack consisting of heart-healthy trail mix and a couple of peanut butter cookies. He strapped on his camelback that contained his water rations for the hike. He exited the stand, switched on his night vision, and began his trek to the cabins.

It was now eleven-thirty as he started down a game trail. The game trail led to a small road that was by one of the abandoned houses to the processing facility. It was quite grown up now but still navigable. Bob was very careful of his footsteps because he did not want to leave any boot prints in any soft areas. He did not want to tip off the contestants about his presence.

The clouds and the moon took turns in defining the walk on his first night to the cabins. It was two and a half miles to his destination, but even in the dark, Bob was able to cover it in about ninety minutes. At different times during his journey, he had the sensation that he was being followed. A couple of times, he thought that he had heard a branch snap. At one point, he even picked up a strange odor. He never could see anything through the night vision, and even stopping to listen, he heard nothing to cause an alarm.

As he closed in on the cabins, Bob left the abandoned road and ventured into the thick foliage to make sure he was not detected. He slipped up a small hill behind the cabins and peered down upon them. After watching for a few seconds, Bob thought, *Great, it's one-ten in the morning. No lights, and everyone's asleep.*

Bob surveyed the cabin for the crew and located his supplies that were set out for him by the crew before they had retired for the night. He planned to sneak down, grab his food supplies, place them on the back side of the hill, and do a little scaring. If all went according to plan, he would be back at the stand by daylight, take a small nap, and maybe be able to interact with some of the contestants in the daylight.

After retrieving his food and placing it on the back side of the hill, Bob returned to his vantage point on top of the hill. As he watched the cabins, he felt the satisfaction of knowing that everything was still in his favor. Once again, without a sound, he managed to descend down to the cabins. He listened closely to make sure there was no activity. He eased around to the front of the contestants' cabin.

Bob quietly climbed the steps, as quietly as one could in tactical boots, and worked his way over to the right side of the cabin. He stealthily peeked into the right-side bedroom window, using the night vision. He could see the room was empty except for some duffel bags. Bob crawled to the left bedroom window and peered in. He looked in and thought to himself, *This is going to be easier than I thought. These eight people are already so scared that they're sleeping in the same room.*

Bob quickly worked out his plan in his head and set it into motion. First, he positioned himself just forward of the window. He thumped the side of the cabin with the palm of his hand. This produced a low thud that could be heard in the bedroom and probably throughout the entire cabin. Bob ran to the steps, taking as long of strides as humanly possible. He bounded down the steps, covering all six in just two moves. He darted by the left side of the cabin to the top of the hill. Even though he heard no movement in the cabin, the plan was successful. As he crouched down and positioned himself toward the cabin, Bob noticed right away that the light was on in the bedroom. In just a matter of seconds, the lights in the kitchen and in the sitting room were on.

*Now, there's some activity happening,* he thought.

\*\*\*

Betty's startled scream awoke the other seven in an instant. After her scream, there was silence. Betty slowly asked, "Did you guys hear that?"

Ronnie was the first to reply. "I heard something running across the deck."

"Before it took off running, it slapped the side of the cabin," Betty said.

"Where did it hit the cabin?" asked Stan.

Betty still had a shocked expression on her face as she pointed and said, "It sounded like...right at our window."

"You mean it may have been looking at us?" asked Sasha.

"I'm not absolutely sure, but that is where it sounded like to me," Betty slowly answered.

Stan and Dave grabbed their flashlights, and Stan said, "Let's take a look."

In the crew cabin, Mark awoke to make his nightly trip to the bathroom. He noticed the lights were on in the other cabin. He rustled around, woke the other crew members, and said, "There must be something going on next door...Better check this out."

The rest of them climbed out of their sleeping bags as Mark turned on the light. They all squinted to shield their eyes and made their way to the door. Just as Stan and Dave came onto the porch, the crew could see their flashlights through the front window. The crew exited the cabin and as-sembled on the side of the deck facing the contestants. By this time, all eight contestants were on the deck and shining their flashlights in every direction.

"What's going on?" Elaine asked.

"There was something on our deck," Sandy answered.

"First, it slapped the side of the cabin, right at our window, and then it ran across the deck," Betty said. "I screamed when I heard the thump, but I think everyone heard it run."

All either verbally agreed or nodded in agreement to what they all heard. They all agreed, whatever it was, it ran across the deck of the cabin.

Up on the small rise, Bob was watching all the commotion down below him with a big grin on his face. He could just barely keep from laughing out loud.

After a few more minutes of discussion, all thirteen decided that whatever it was, it obviously had vacated the area and probably would not come back around. Everybody returned to their respective cabins, but the women contestants insisted that Dave lock the door. They insisted that Stan check it to be sure. Both men did this without any hesitation. They decided that the kitchen light should stay on for the rest of the night. They returned to the bedroom.

As the crew shut the cabin door and locked it, Elaine asked, "Did either one of you carry a gun outside just now?"

Bill and Mark looked at each other, smiled, and simply nodded no.

Elaine smiled and said, "Some protectors you guys are. What if there had been a bear outside?"

"If a bear had attacked everyone outside just now and we started shooting, one of us might have shot one of the contestants. Better for the bear to weed out the weak than one of us," Mark said.

They all laughed. "Hey, let's check the monitor and see where Bob is. I'll bet it was him," Tim said.

"And by the way, Elaine, if you remember, Rob did tell us to be sure and not shoot Bob," Bill added. "Remember?"

Once again, they all laughed. Andre picked up the monitor and pushed the power button. After a couple of seconds, the screen came into view.

"Yep, there's Bob, the ole expert outdoorsman," Andre said with a grin. "He's on the hill right behind the cabins. He's close enough to throw a rock at us."

"I bet he got a kick out of watching us," Bill said and chuckled.

"No doubt," Andre said. "But I would like to be a fly on the wall next door and listen to the conversation in that bedroom."

"I can only imagine what's going through their minds," Elaine added.

The crew turned out the lights as they worked their way back to the bedroom. Everybody climbed back into their sleeping bags. Tim turned out the bedroom light. As he walked to his bunk, he glanced out the window and said, "This camping trip may be over pretty soon. I think these people are getting a little jumpy."

"Why's that?" Mark asked.

"Well, first off, they all settled in one bedroom," Tim said. "And now it appears like they are going to sleep with the kitchen light on."

"Ole Bob did a good job tonight," Mark laughed.

By the time everyone settled back down, it was about four in the morning. Bob decided to head back to the stand, fix a hot meal, and get some rest. He was very careful not to step on any soft ground. He figured that once it got light, the contestants would be out snooping around. The hike back was gratifying after a good night's work. It was a short night but a good one, nonetheless. This time, Bob didn't have any strange sensations and didn't hear anything out of the ordinary. Back in the stand, he cooked his food, ate, climbed in his sleeping bag, and dozed off.

Back at the crew cabin, Andre awoke suddenly.

*Did I hear something or was I dreaming?* he thought.

He didn't bother to check the time and just lay there quietly. It was still dark outside, so he figured he hadn't been back asleep very long. He heard it again. *I wasn't dreaming,* he thought. *That sounded like a small pebble hitting the roof of the cabin.*

A few seconds passed, and there it was again. This time it struck the back side of the cabin. Andre thought, *Ole Bob is not finished with the tricks tonight, but why is he throwing them at our cabin? Surely, he knows we are in on the game. Rob had to have told him this...I'm sure he did.*

Andre continued to lay there and listen. Everything was quiet and calm.

*Okay, Bob, go get some rest. We'll see you tomorrow*, he thought. After a few minutes, he faded off to sleep. Little did Andre know that Bob was back at the stand and had been there for over an hour.

# CHAPTER 6

As the darkness gave way to the morning light, all the clouds had moved out of the area. It had all the appearance of being a beautiful day. Soon after the sun began to rise, the water droplets on the plants began to glisten as the rays peeked through the trees. The water on the bay was as slick as glass and was only interrupted by a mother whale and her calf breaching the surface periodically.

Betty was the first to rise this morning. She couldn't sleep for more than fifteen minutes at a time because of hearing that thump on the cabin. She ambled over to the bedroom window. She stared into an endless, dark void, even though it was daylight and the crew cabin was right next door.

The next to awaken was Sandy. She rubbed her eyes and immediately saw Betty standing at the window. As she slid out of her sleeping bag, Betty turned to look at Sandy but said nothing.

Sandy walked over to Betty and put her hand on Betty's shoulder. "You okay?"

Betty glanced over at Sandy, then turned back to look out the window and said, "I think so. But you know...the longer we're here at this place, it is starting to give me the creeps."

Sandy patted Betty on her shoulder and said, "Last night was a little scary, I have to admit. But I've been thinking about what Sasha asked last night." She paused a second and asked, "Do you think something might have actually been looking in the window at us?"

"I don't know, but why else would it have walked over to it?" Betty answered.

Sandy looked out the window, then back at Betty and said, "Probably just a hungry ole bear looking for a way in to grab an easy meal. Maybe he smelled the hamburgers we cooked for supper."

Betty looked down at the floor. "Yeah, maybe, but it sure didn't sound like a bear when it ran across the deck. It sounded more like a man. At least, I think it did." Betty looked back up and said, "It's hard to say for sure. I was sound asleep when whatever it was startled me. Hopefully, we can figure it out today."

One by one, the others awakened and crawled out of their sleeping bags. It didn't appear that anyone got a good night's sleep after they had all settled back down. No others talked about the restless night, especially the men. Their macho sides paved the way for their braveness this morning.

Stan stretched and said, "Alright, the sun is shining this morning. I hope that means no rain today. It's going to be a good day to check out the area a little more, and maybe we can figure out what that was last night."

Dave chimed in, "Oh, yeah, I'm ready to do some exploring. Let's see if we can find some evidence of this so-called Hairy Man."

Betty glanced back at Sandy and grinned. "Men. I bet if that thing last night was sitting at the firepit this morning, they would invite it in for breakfast."

Sandy smiled and said, "They probably would."

Shelley was the first to enter the front area of the cabin, and right away she noticed that the crew was on their deck drinking coffee. "Looks like the crew were early to rise this morning. How about we start some breakfast?"

"Let me holler at the crew," Willy offered. Willy opened the door and met the crew with a hearty wave. "Everybody ready to eat?"

The crew turned, chuckled, and welcomed Willy's invitation. Each of them grabbed their coffee cups and made their way to the contestants' cabin. In single file, they climbed the steps and followed Willy through the door.

Andre cleared the last step and glanced to his left to see if the pebble was still lying there from the day before. Not only was it still there, but now there were two of them on the railing, lying side by side. The second one was not as large as the first but perfectly round. He paused to study the stones. He had the sensation that the stones were not the only thing being studied. He felt someone or something was watching him.

Andre slowly turned in a circular motion and carefully peered into the surrounding foliage. There was nothing to be seen, or was there? He saw a dark spot behind the cabins just in the tree line at the top of the hill. He thought, *If there is something there, it's not moving.*

He stared at it. Must be just shadows from the morning light shining through the trees.

Mark interrupted Andre's thoughts when he asked him if he was coming inside. Andre jumped, turned to Mark, and smiled. He followed Mark into the cabin. Once inside, Andre heard all the contestants and some of the crew discussing last night's events — the thump and the sound of something running across the deck. Even though the crew knew about Bob, they played along gracefully. It was obvious that there was something bothering Andre. Andre just couldn't get those stones out of his mind.

After breakfast was prepared and everyone sat down to eat, the conversation dwindled. Mostly all that was heard was the occasional clanging of silverware on the plates and the sound of coffee cups being placed back in their resting places.

Shelley finished her plate and leaned back in her chair to savor the rest of her coffee when something caught her eye. With the direction of the morning light and the difference of the angle sitting in her chair, she noticed something on the window itself.

She thought, *Is that a handprint? A smudge?* Whatever it was, it didn't appear to belong there. Shelley slowly got out of her chair, took her plate and utensils to the sink, and picked up her coffee cup. With the cup in tow, she ambled over to the window and began to study it. Something was on the outside of the glass. She thought, *If that is a handprint, it's enormous.* Even though she could not determine what was on the outside of the window glass, she knew that it didn't belong there. She didn't recall any of them being near that window at any time.

After they cleaned the dishes and straightened up the morning mess, Bill asked, "Okay, guys and gals, what's on the agenda for the day?"

They all discussed the agenda for the day for a few minutes and decided they were going to split into two separate groups. They would explore in different directions to see what they could find. Searching the shoreline for what Betty had seen would just have to wait.

"Great!" Mark said. "Bill can go with one group, and I will go with the other. We'll follow and do some field filming of the groups for the show. Give us about twenty minutes to dress for the hike and to grab our gear."

The crew returned to their cabin. Andre paused and took a snapshot of the pebbles.

Once back in the cabin, Andre said, "Hey, guys." He paused. Everyone looked at Andre with puzzled expressions. "Has anyone else noticed the rocks on the railing of the other cabin?"

"What are you talking about, Andre?" Bill asked.

"The first morning after we arrived here, when we wandered over to the other cabin to eat breakfast, at the top of the steps to the left, there was a single pebble sitting on the railing," Andre said.

"And?" Bill said.

"Well, this morning there's another stone, a little smaller, lying right beside the first," Andre continued. "Like they were placed there."

"Maybe Mr. Long put them there," Elaine interjected.

"That's possible, but he didn't arrive until noon on the second day," Andre replied.

"Alright, guys, what are we talking about here?" Elaine asked. "Could one of the contestants have placed them there?"

"Maybe," Tim said. "If they are like the small stones down at the shoreline, they were down there both the first and second day, so one of them may have picked them up for souvenirs."

"Maybe that's how one of them is keeping count of the days that we are here," Mark said.

"That sounds reasonable, but why leave them on the railing? Why not take them inside?" Tim asked.

"Should we say something to them or just wait to see if more stones appear tomorrow?" Andre asked.

"Let's wait and see," Mark answered. "No use in spreading rumors till we know a little more."

Suddenly, the SAT Phone came to life and rang. Everyone in the room jumped and started laughing.

Mark answered the phone, still chuckling. "Good morning, Rob."

"How did you know it was me, ole boy?" Rob asked.

"Who else would call us on this phone?" Mark said.

"I guess you had a fifty-fifty shot of whether it was me or Mr. Long. How did it go last night?" Rob said.

"Mr. Bob Long paid us a visit last night," Mark answered. "I'm pretty sure he made an impression on the contestants, and his supplies were gone this morning."

"Wonderful," Rob said. "Oh, by the way, see if the techs can look at the remote camera at the other cabin. We couldn't get any signal from it last night. Don't let the others know it's there."

"Roger that, boss. Anything else?" Mark said.

"Nope, that should about do it," Rob answered. "I'll call back to check in and get some good footage for me."

Then the line went dead, and Mark looked at Tim and said, "See, it's nothing personal. Rob's just not too savvy at phone conversations."

Tim just shook his head.

Earlier, the day before, Tim had found four walkie talkies in the technicians' supply boxes. "I found these yesterday — a surprise that Rob forgot to inform us of so we can keep in touch with these. Since you will be splitting into two groups, each group can carry one, and if anyone needs medical attention, you can holler, and Elaine will come running."

Elaine turned on a dime and asked in a raised tone, "By myself?"

Tim grinned and said, "No, Andre and I will escort you."

Elaine pointed her finger at Tim and said, "That's more like it."

The crew opened the door and walked out onto the deck. The contestants had already assembled at the bottom of the steps and were waiting patiently. It had been closer to thirty minutes, but Mark and Bill were finally ready.

Dave spoke first. "We've divided into our groups and are all ready for the scouting trip, men." He gave the cameramen a two-finger salute up against his forehead.

Bill and Mark looked at each other and gave the two-finger, and the other seven followed suit with a two-finger salute. Mark and Bill walked down the steps, and they took a small path to the old, abandoned road above the cabins.

As they got there, Bill said, "Okay, people, we will follow your lead and film from behind. Periodically, we will film from the front. I guess the best thing for the show is for you guys to pretend we are not here. And make sure that there is film footage from your cameras. Try not to get us in it, though. If you do, I'm sure the people at the network can edit it out."

All agreed. The contestants had already discussed their plan for the hike and clued the cameramen in on their plans.

The first group consisted of Dave, Willy, Sasha, Betty, and Mark. The second group consisted of Stan, Ronnie, Shelley, Sandy, and Bill. The two groups wished each other good luck, and they were off.

The first group simply started down to the left and the others to the right. Tim, Andre, and Elaine stood leaning on the deck railing and watched them slowly disappear in each direction. They could still hear the groups talking, but nobody was visible in the thick brush. After just a minute or two, there were no human sounds — just the sounds of the forest and the birds chirping all around them.

Elaine was the first to break the silence and said, "After the conversations about the pebbles and the grunting sound down the shoreline, I kind of wish we had a weapon also."

Tim smiled at her and said, "Don't worry, Elaine. It just so happens that we do."

Andre looked at Tim. "You bring a gun?" he asked.

"Yes, I did," Tim said. "I wasn't coming out here in the wilderness with this so-called Hairy Man without one. I hid it in one of our bags we carried ashore. Would now be a good time to retrieve it?"

"Absolutely. Do you think we should tell Mark and Bill?" Andre asked.

"Well, remember, no secrets among the crew," Tim said. "I think they will understand, especially since the three of us are going to be stuck here at the cabin by ourselves a lot of the time."

The three of them entered the cabin, and Elaine instinctively locked the door. *Just in case,* she thought. *Maybe I'm being a little silly, or maybe not. Anyway, it makes me feel better to turn the deadbolt.*

Tim found the bag again, unzipped it, and removed the pistol. When Elaine caught sight of the gun, she felt a small rush of security run through her veins, even though she had not fired guns that much. Her dad had been a hunter for as long as she could remember, but she had never shown much interest in sitting out in the woods, freezing to death for entertainment. She listened to his stories about his hunting adventures, and even found them very interesting, but she just didn't have the desire to brave the elements. It would be nice for him to be here now to make her feel a little more secure.

As Tim zipped up the bag, the SAT Phone rang.

"Hello?" Tim answered.

Mr. Long responded in a deep and raspy voice, "Hey, guys, this is Bob Long."

"Good morning, Mr. Long. How can I help you?" Tim asked.

"First off, I wanted to know how I did last night, and secondly, I wanted to know what the contestants' plans are for the day," Bob answered. "If I know where they are, I might be able to add some excitement for them today."

"Last night did leave an impression on them," Tim said. "They just left minutes ago on the old, abandoned road to start exploring the area. Half of the group took a left, and the others went right."

"I guess I had better get my act together," Bob said. "Thanks a bunch. Goodbye, guys."

"Goodbye," Tim said.

Tim looked up at Elaine and Andre and said, "At least Bob knows how to properly end a phone conversation." He raised to his feet and added, "Now that everyone is gone, let's check on that remote camera next door."

The three of them walked over to the cabin and entered the door. It took a little searching, but Andre finally found the hiding spot for the camera. They checked the camera and the wiring to it. The power to the camera was on, the small green light on the back of it was flashing properly, and the video line was also secure. They traced the video line down the trim on the cabin wall, and it was also well hidden. It entered a closet and traveled through a small conduit pipe to a disconnect on the outside wall.

"Power is good, and video line is okay in here," Andre said. "Must be a problem outside or where it ties into the transmitter box in our cabin."

The troubleshooting inside the cabin didn't take more than thirty minutes to achieve. The three of them went outside to check the cable. They started down the steps when suddenly, they stopped as if they were frozen in their tracks. They all noticed something at the same time.

"Oh my gosh!" Elaine said. "What in the world is that smell? It smells like something dead."

"Maybe it is," Tim said. "A bear may have killed something close by. Let's hurry up and check this cable. We don't want to be added to the lunch menu."

The three hurriedly moved between the cabins and found the disconnect. The problem became evident as soon as they found the cable. The cable and its connector had been ripped out of the side of the cabin. That could have been repairable by the techs, but there were two other sections of the cable that were torn or chewed apart. Not only was the cable in three pieces, but one section appeared to be missing altogether. The techs did not have any extra cable. It was a lost cause for repairing the video for the contestant's cabin.

With nothing they could do to fix the issue with the video cable, the three of them collectively decided to retreat back to their cabin. They navigated through the small undergrowth between the cabins and reached the safety of their deck. They all stopped and surveyed the perimeter of the cabins. The smell was still very much evident and was easily detected no matter which direction one was looking. There was an uneasy feeling that came over the three of them as they entered the door.

Andre stopped short of the door to take another quick glance around. Something caught his eye. He thought, *How did I miss that when we exited the contestants' cabin?* Right there on the deck railing were not one, not two, but several pebbles placed all in a row.

"Hey, people, take a look at this," Andre said and pointed.

Elaine and Tim were already standing in the sitting room when they heard Andre speak. "What is it?" Elaine asked. She and Tim headed back outside.

"The two stones on the railing..." Andre began. "Well, they have grown in number. Did either of you notice it when we came out of the cabin?"

"I never paid any attention when we came out. How many are there now?" Tim asked.

"I'm not sure. We need to take a look and see," Andre said.

Elaine and Tim followed Andre to the edge of their deck. Nothing was spoken for a few seconds.

"I count fourteen in all. How about you guys?" Andre asked.

"That's how many I got. There goes the theory that a contestant was counting our days here," Tim joked.

"Andre, are you absolutely sure there was only one stone yesterday and just two this morning?" Elaine asked.

"I'm positive," Andre insisted. "When we left breakfast this morning, I even took a picture of the stones, and there were only two of them."

"Then how do you explain fourteen of them now?" Tim asked.

"I don't have a clue, but something put those stones there," Andre replied. "They're all placed in a neatly arranged row."

"Maybe whatever is making that smell put them on the railing," Elaine said. "It would've had to do it when we were inside checking the cable. We were in there for probably a half an hour or so. There would have been time to put them there."

"It couldn't have been Bob. We just talked to him on the SAT Phone," Tim said.

"Maybe there is something here, guys. But what is the message with the rocks?" Andre asked.

Elaine turned to face Andre and Tim, and for split second she was sure she got a glimpse of something move on the hill above the cabin. She gasped slightly and adjusted her feet on the deck. This startled the other two. They gave a quick glance at Elaine and was surprised to see her blank stare.

"What's the matter, Elaine?" Tim asked with a tone of concern.

Elaine paused and after a couple of seconds said, "I could have sworn that I saw something move up on the hill. This place is starting to give me the creeps with the rocks being thrown, the terrible smell, and now the pebbles. Someone or something doesn't want us here. I think all of these things are signs."

"I'm not sure what is going on, but I think we should keep a close eye on each other and monitor our surroundings at all times," Tim said. "We'll talk with Mark and Bill tonight after supper to see what they think, okay?"

"Sounds good to me," Andre said. "I'd like to get their opinion on all of this before we jump to any conclusions. Let's all go inside, listen for the walkie talkies, and make sure nobody needs our assistance during their excursions today."

They all agreed and walked back into the cabin. Andre locked the door securely. Elaine and Tim noted that he locked the door, but none of them felt secure.

# CHAPTER 7

The old, abandoned road was nothing more than an overgrown trail in most places, but for some reason there seemed to be a path that was easily walkable for most of the newcomers who had recently come to the area.

Occasionally, one had to duck under an overhanging branch or dodge a protruding limb that seemed to aim directly at a person's head. The path was well worn, down to the dirt in most places, which made Mark wonder just how much wildlife roamed this trail. He wondered if there was a possibility the group might encounter something they didn't necessarily want to meet.

He thought, *Should we be making more noise to alert the animals of their presence?*

He remembered a documentary he watched, and in the show, the hikers were directed to have two pots tied to their backpacks, clanging against each other to alert bears of their presence. The show filmed a bear leaving the trail and sitting behind a scrub bush, and after watching the hikers pass by him, he simply came back to the trail and continued on his way. But Mark hoped that the conversations of the group were enough to do the job to keep away unwanted encounters.

The group moved at what Mark considered to be a snail's pace, carefully scouring the sides of the trail and the brush that surrounded it. They appeared to be seriously checking for any evidence they might be able to uncover to prove there was truly something that inhabited this place. Mark filmed the group in the tight confines of the trail as best he could. Dave and Betty suddenly came to a stop in their tracks.

"Hey, guys, look at this," Dave said to the group, pointing to a branch. "This branch has been broken recently. It's still green around the splintered section."

"There's an impression in the moss. Something has moved through here," Betty added.

"What do you suppose it was, a bear maybe?" Willy asked.

"I don't think so," Sasha said. "The break is pretty high up on the sapling, unless he was standing on his back legs and reaching for berries."

"I don't see any berries around the break," Betty said. "It looks like it was broken as whatever moved through the area. Let's document it with our cameras and then take a closer look in the underbrush behind it."

Dave filmed the impression and the broken branch, and the four of them eased through the area behind their discovery. Unfortunately, there was nothing else to be seen, and they decided to continue down the trail.

*Pretty good detective work by the group*, Mark thought. *This was probably the work of Bob as he approached the cabins last night...Still, that is impressive.*

They walked down the trail, and the brush began to transform into more of a vast forest. The trees seemed to touch the sky, and the shining light that illuminated the path became less and less. Nobody spoke much at all, and if they did, it was in a low whisper. Everyone walked slowly and scanned the forest. All that could be seen were several small birds darting from tree to tree, and the occasional squirrel jumping from branch to branch.

Just ahead, the group could see that the sun was shining bright. They walked through the opening at the edge of the forest. They came into a small clearing, which most likely was where one of the workers lived. Though it had grown up a lot with small saplings, it was obvious that this once had been a homestead at the port. Right in the middle of the clearing was what remained of the home, and beside of that was what appeared to be an out-door storage area, which probably stored tools and equipment.

The team began to search the area for clues. They weren't exactly sure what it was they were looking for, but nonetheless they eagerly searched. At the shed, after moving a few small boards, they did find several tools. Some of the tools were rusted, and some of the wooden handles exposed to the elements had deteriorated completely.

They made their way to what was left of the house. There were only three walls still standing; the roof and one wall had partially collapsed. They observed the inside, and all noticed that the furniture was still there, including the pots and pans that occupied the kitchen area. Metal drinking cups still remained on the counter, and the spices were still sitting on what was left of the spice rack.

"So, when these people left, they apparently traveled light," Willy said. "Looks like they took nothing with them. Were they really in this big of a hurry to get out?"

"Why would you not take your belongings with you as you go?" Dave interjected. "That doesn't make any sense."

"Most men I know might leave a few things, but never their tools," Sasha said.

"According to legend, this so-called Hairy Man had the inhabitants scared to death, but did the men not have weapons?" Betty said. "I've never seen a situation where men were in the wilderness without weapons. That just doesn't seem possible, especially in this remote area."

They began to move around the outside of the cabin, and something caught Sasha's eye. She stopped and studied what she was seeing. It looked out of place, lying beside the end of the counter. It was an off-white color and partially covered by an old rocking chair that had toppled over many years ago.

She slowly entered the space between the roof and the remnants of the standing wall that were supporting it. She moved closer, and it became evident what she was looking at. Sasha let out a large gasp and took a couple steps back. Dave rounded the corner and heard her breathing as he reached for her arm.

"What's the matter, Sasha? You okay?" asked Dave.

"Over there, at the end of the counter under the rocker, there's a skull," Sasha slowly murmured.

"What?" Betty screamed.

Marked filmed Dave and Willy quickly moving around to the edge of the counter to take a look. She was correct. It was a human skull. The left side of the skull appeared to be slightly caved in from a hard fall or a blow to the head. There was nothing around the skull that could have done this kind of damage.

Dave scanned around. He found more bones scattered throughout the room. Accompanying the skull was an assortment of bones between the counter and the wall. That didn't really make sense to Dave unless small critters had moved the bones in their quest for a meal. But the bones that made up the left arm were located in a totally different area from the right arm, and both were nowhere close to the skull.

*Where are this poor individual's legs?* he thought. After a few more minutes of looking, Dave spotted the legs on the other side of the room. He carefully moved through the debris to the left of the floor, and it appeared to be another entrance to the house. *Yup, these are leg bones.*

Dave looked at the others and cautiously said, "It looks like this person was torn apart. What in the world happened here?"

For a few seconds, there was just silence. Sasha and Betty didn't even offer an answer to Dave's question.

Willy finally quit surveying the cabin floor and looked up to break the silence. "Do all of these bones belong to the same person or are there multiple people here?"

"I believe they are all one person," Dave responded.

"Then why are they scattered throughout the house?" Sasha asked.

"At first, I thought they had been scattered around by small animals eating on the remains, but now I'm not so sure," Dave said. "Why is the rocking chair turned over? And it appears that this door near the leg bones has been ripped off its hinges. I'm not sure what went on here."

Dave and Willy filmed all they could inside the cabin. The women decided to log the outside features with their cameras while Mark caught the group's activities on his camera.

They all decided to head back to the cabins and see what the other group had found. The group slowly made their way back to the trail. The group was unaware that they were being watched all the time by an outsider. Bob had positioned himself above the group, just inside the tree line, so he could follow them when they made their way back to the trail.

They kept discussing what they had discovered. They discussed what might have happened at this house. They slowly inched back up the trail when a good-sized rock came crashing down the mountainside.

At first, the group believed something was running towards them. They were startled. Mark, once again, instinctively placed his hand on the gun hid at his side. The rock bounced out from a downed tree and crossed the trail in front of them. They immediately turned their attention to the hill. Nobody could see anything in the trees above them. They stood frozen without any movement for several minutes. They watched ever so intently, hoping to see something move, but nothing moved in the forest.

"A rock just doesn't dislodge and crash down the mountainside like that!" Willy said excitedly. "That's the second time that has happened, people."

"Just like the rock at the shoreline when the others were up above the processing facility," Dave added with a fearful tone. "It came crashing down from above them."

After several minutes of staring into the forest above them, the group moved along the trail. This time, they walked at a faster pace; however, there were no more surprises for them.

During the time that the group investigated the house down the trail, the other group moved up the old, abandoned road and made their way around the hillside to what appeared to be a large valley at the end of the bay. They could see through the small gaps in the trees a large flat grassy area with a good-sized stream flowing into the bay. It took several minutes to walk and reach the edge of what they had been viewing. When they arrived, all of them stood there in awe.

"This place is gorgeous. I don't believe I have ever seen anything like it," Sandy said.

"Absolutely beautiful! It would be a great place for a house just up there in the edge of the woods overlooking the bay," Shelley added.

"Yeah, but it would be a long way to the grocery store," Stan said.

All laughed as they stood, taking in the beauty of the view.

"Is this the stream where the body parts were found by the lady that worked at the facility?" Ronnie asked.

"Well, there went the idea of a nice house in the woods overlooking the bay," Shelley said and snickered.

They all chuckled.

"I believe this is probably the one described in the paperwork that we all received. Everyone up for taking a look?" Stan asked.

Everybody nodded. They eased down the bank onto the shore and started making their way to the stream. The grass that bordered the stream was probably waist deep, and nobody was eager to trek through it. As they got to the mouth of the stream, they noticed several paths worn through the grass in all directions.

"Seems to be a lot of wildlife activity traveling through this area," Stan said. "Probably the local bears coming down to the stream to fish."

"We keep talking about the deer and the bears, but why don't we see more of them?" Shelley asked.

"Maybe they are keeping their distance and trying to figure out just what we are," Stan answered. "I have noticed some tracks left behind by both. But come to think of it, I haven't noticed as many as I expected."

As they talked, there was a noticeable sudden aroma that alarmed each person. It smelled musky and reeked of dead flesh. Everyone looked around in hopes of identifying the sudden smell that penetrated their noses, but no animal was seen.

Shelley noticed that across the stream, the blades of grass were moving, but in the direction away from them. It appeared to be something large but was not visible above the grass. She did not speak and raised her hand and pointed at the movement. The others quickly looked in the direction of the swaying grass.

They were standing too low to see into the grass. Whatever it was continued through the grass to the tree line and just disappeared without a trace. The group stood silent. Wide eyed, they glanced at each other as if to make sure everyone else witnessed what just happened.

Sandy was the first to break the silence. "What did we just see, people?" she asked.

"Maybe we just interrupted a local bear's fishing trip, but I've never known a bear that smelled that way," Stan said. "Have you noticed that the smell diminished after that thing left? Wait right here, guys. Let me cross this stream and take a look. When I get over there, make sure I'm at the right place."

Stan waded the cool, clear water of the stream. He climbed out of the bank on the other side and eased through the grass toward the direction of the movement. The others offered directions as he closed in on the spot. He suddenly stopped, turned, and looked at them.

"What do you see?" Ronnie yelled.

"There's really nothing here except a large area matted down like a bedding area," Stan yelled.

"A bedding area for what?" Sandy asked.

"I'm not really sure. I'm going to get some footage of this and come back over," Stan said.

In about half the time it took Stan to get to the spot, he returned to the others. He turned around every now and glanced behind him.

"What did you see, Stan?" Shelley asked with curiosity.

"What looked like a bedding area, but it was different. It didn't look like a bear or deer impression. It almost looked like I had laid down there," Stan said.

"Like something that walks on two legs...is what you're saying?" Ronnie asked slowly.

"Yeah, it was strange. I could have laid down beside it and made almost the same impression," Stan confirmed.

"What do you mean almost?" Sandy asked.

Stan looked at Sandy and said, "Well, my impression would not have been as large as it was. It...it was much bigger than I am."

"Maybe we should go back over there and compare one of us to it. We'll need something to show the size of it," Ronnie said seriously.

They all agreed.

Stan and Ronnie crossed the stream and waded through the grass to the bed. Ronnie was amazed when he saw the matted down grass. He was larger than Stan, so he decided to volunteer to lay in the grassy bed. Stan shot the video of Ronnie lying in the bedding area. Both men were amazed at how big this thing must have been. They returned to the edge of the stream and waded back across.

The others anxiously waited for them to return.

"So, how big was this thing, and what do you think it was, Ronnie?" Sandy quickly asked.

Ronnie looked Sandy in the eyes and said, "It was bigger than Stan or me. But it sure looked like one of us had been laying there."

"If that's what we saw moving through the grass, and it is that big, how come we never actually saw the animal or whatever it was?" Shelley asked in a matter-of-fact tone.

"I don't know," Stan said with a hint of fear. "Maybe it was crawling through the grass, or maybe it didn't want us to see it. We could have seen another animal running through the grass, so what we saw might not have made that impression. It is something manlike that has been lying in that exact spot, though. And if it were lying there, I'm not sure I want to see it standing up that close to us."

Bill filmed the entire episode of the group's encounter with whatever ran through the tall grass. Bill, too, had an uneasy feeling about the situation.

"We had better start back to make sure we get there before dark," Bill instructed. "I don't want to be out here after the sun goes down...especially after this little incident."

They headed back around the shoreline and climbed back up to the abandoned road where they were earlier. They paused for a second to catch their breath. That's when they heard the *whoop* from across the grassy area at the mouth of the valley.

Everyone stood very still and listened. The second *whoop* came from the top of the mountain above them. They heard a low grunt coming from the tree line where the "thing" had disappeared after moving through the grass. Bill never hit the stop button on his camera, and all three sounds were captured on audio. They listened for another five minutes, but the grunting sound stopped, and the only sounds were the birds chirping in the woods.

Sandy broke the silence and said, "Let's get a move on, people. I'm not going to get caught out here with whatever that was after dark."

Nobody acknowledged her verbally, but all turned and headed back down the trail to the safety of the cabins. There was no conversation among them as they walked. Each person was sorting through their own thoughts of what had just taken place, yet none of them had a clear explanation of the events.

As they got to the cabins, they noticed the others had beaten them there. There was a lot of activity on the deck of the crew cabin. Several people were talking at the same time, and the conversations could not be understood.

Everybody on the deck stopped talking at once and peered at the group as they walked up.

"Did you guys have any luck?" Dave asked.

"I suppose you can call it luck, but we are not one hundred percent sure of exactly what we discovered," Stan said.

"Sounds like our luck today," Sasha said. "How about we compare information tonight at supper? Maybe we can make some sense of everything as a group — at least, I hope we can. Let's get cleaned up, fix some grub, and try to figure some of this out."

Everyone nodded in agreement and slowly headed to their respective cabins.

Once inside their cabin, Andre asked, "I'm guessing both groups had a little excitement today?"

Bill and Mark looked at the other. "There were some interesting events that occurred for both groups," Mark said.

Elaine agreed and informed them that they were not the only ones that experienced strange events that day.

As the cameramen began to put the equipment away, Tim announced, "I think we should talk, just the five of us. There's some strange things going on here."

Mark looked up and said, "We found something very interesting down the trail. I believe it was at one of the original workers' homes. Also, we experienced some more rock throwing. I guess the rock might have been compliments of our friend Bob, but whatever happened in that cabin, Mr. Long had nothing to do with it."

"Bob could not have been in two places at once," Bill said. "We found an imprint in the tall grass of the meadow at the head of the bay. We also saw something moving through the grass. It remained in a crouched position as it escaped to the woods."

"What did the imprint look like?" Elaine asked.

Bill shook his head and replied, "It was strange. It looked like a very large man had been lying there, but this would have meant that the man was much larger than any of us. Plus, we heard a couple of weird vocalizations, and they came from two entirely different areas. It was almost like two animals were trying to communicate with each other. They sounded like a *whoop* noise. The sounds were loud, and we all clearly heard them."

"Well, the video for the other cabin is a bust," Andre said. "The coax cable has been torn out of the junction box of the contestants' cabin. And by the way, some of the cable is completely missing, and there's nothing we can do to repair it. There's one more thing..." Andre paused for Bill and Mark's reactions.

Bill and Mark stood there staring at Andre, waiting for him to continue. Andre looked them in the eye and continued. "The rocks on the porch railing? Now, there's fourteen of them lying there."

"The three of you were here all day, so how did they get there?" Bill asked, puzzled.

"We think they were placed there when we were checking on the remote camera problem in the other cabin," Tim said. "And there was a terrible odor in the air when we came outside. Sort of like something had been close by."

"I believe I saw something on the hill behind us," Elaine added. "I can't be sure, but it appeared that something moved and disappeared to the other side in the brush."

Andre looked at the group and announced, "I don't think we are alone here, guys."

"How alone is what concerns me," Mark said with fear in his voice.

"Let's get supper finished and discuss this some more in private when we get back over here," Bill said.

Bill and Mark cleaned up, and the five of them headed to the other cabin. This time, there was no one waiting on the deck to greet them, so after climbing the steps, Andre, who was in the lead, stopped. He casually pointed to the stones, which were placed neatly in a row. Bill and Mark counted the stones silently.

Andre opened the door to what almost sounded like a small social party going on, except there was no music playing. It was just the sound of eight people all talking at once, describing the day's events. The contestants barely noticed the crew entering the cabin. Elaine watched closely as Tim shut and locked the door.

Stan was detailing the manner the grass moved as "whatever it was" escaped the meadow. He and Ronnie described the imprint and how large it actually was. Shelley would chime in every now and then to tell them about the *whooping* sounds they all heard. The other group was busy telling about the bone fragments and skull they found at the partially collapsed house down the trail. Some added the fact that another rock had been thrown at them.

The crew looked at each other and Bill said, "Sounds like it's been a pretty exciting day for everyone. I'm not sure we can get them to calm down enough to fix this meal."

"We may have to fix supper all by ourselves. Let's get started, I'm starving," Elaine concluded.

Soon, everyone settled down just enough to prepare some food. They all opted for soup and sandwiches since it was an easy meal and there was a lot for everyone to talk about tonight. The contestants never stopped rambling on about all they had discovered, heard, and saw during the day. There were more questions than answers. Mark set a camera on the lamp table to catch them as they ate. The crew mainly just listened to the conversation and only interjected when asked a question about the day's activities. The three that stayed behind told nothing about the stones or the odor they encountered at the cabins.

Bill and Mark took turns filming the group after the meal was over and they had finished eating. All thirteen sat around and enjoyed a cup of coffee. The crew listened as the other eight discussed their plan for the next day's exploring and what they needed to look for. Not long after they emptied their cups and the dishes were put away, the crew called it a night and headed back to their cabin.

# CHAPTER 8

O nce the crew was back in the cabin with the door securely locked, they began to talk. All decided on another round of coffee, and each one discussed their concerns over the situation at the port.

Elaine quickly asked the first question. "Mark, I heard the others mentioning bone fragments. Just what did you guys find in that homestead?"

"I'm not sure what happened there or when it took place, but I do believe it was violent," Mark answered. "The side door to the house had been kicked in and was lying on the inside. The hinges were still attached to the door facing, but the door itself looked like the screws had been ripped out of it. In the kitchen at the end of the counter, there was a rocking chair lying on its side, and beside the chair was a skull along with several bone fragments. I didn't see the arm and leg bones. Dave began to look around, and soon more bones were found, and they appeared to be the arms and legs of this individual. The bones were scattered in various areas of the room."

"You mean the arms and legs were nowhere near the skull?" Elaine asked calmly.

"Exactly. Either something had moved the bones or this person...had been torn apart. Also, all the tools were still in the shed, the supplies still in the cabin, and I think whoever this person was must have met their demise before they ever tried to escape this place."

"When did the group have the rock thrown at them?" Tim asked.

Mark looked at Tim and replied, "It was on the way back, but maybe the rock was from Bob because we never could see anything up in the woods. But whatever happened in that house, I'm sure Bob Long had nothing to do with it. I would like to take another look inside that cabin just to check it out more closely."

Mark turned to Bill and asked, "What all did your crew see out there?"

Bill took a sip of coffee and lowered his cup. "I really don't know. When the grass was moving, I could get a glimpse of a dark figure every now and then. At first, I thought that we had just spooked a bear and it was trying to avoid us. But the impression in the meadow was definitely not made by a bear, and the *whooping* sound couldn't have been a bear either. And the odor was terrible."

"What was the odor like?" Andre asked.

"It's hard to explain. It was kind of like rotting flesh, musky...Oh, I don't know. It was not pleasant at all," Bill replied.

"Sounds like the same kind of smell we encountered here, just before we noticed the stones, and Elaine saw something on the hill behind the cabins," Tim said.

"I don't understand the rocks," Mark said. "How come there was one, then two, then fourteen? That doesn't make any sense at all, and none of the contestants have mentioned them."

"Do you think it's possible they haven't noticed them yet?" Andre asked.

"I suppose so. I hadn't seen them until you pointed them out," Bill replied.

"I know we are supposed to show a little fear to make this seem realistic to those eight people over there, but a feeling inside tells me there is really something here," Elaine said apprehensively. "I don't believe small cuts and abrasions are the main concern. Could this Hairy Man be for real?"

Mark looked back at Bill and asked, "What was the trail like to the meadow that your group found?"

"Strangely, it was well worn and appeared to be traveled quite frequently," Bill answered.

"The trail to the homestead was exactly the same way, even though every now and then, a person would have to duck to miss a branch," Mark said. "But in some places, it was worn down to the dirt."

"What about the construction crew building the cabins?" Elaine asked.

"What do you mean?" Bill asked.

"Did they have any strange occurrences while they were here?" Elaine asked.

"If they did, Rob didn't mention it. I'm assuming that they were only on the land during the day and probably slept on the boat at night," Mark answered.

"Maybe that's why it's coming around now. We're here twenty-four hours a day, just like the workers in the fishing village," Andre said.

"It might have been checking this place out then, but if the construction crew were sleeping on the boat, they wouldn't have had any encounters," Tim said. "I think we should get a little more information before we talk to Rob. I'd hate to ruin the big show before it gets started."

Mark nodded his head in agreement. "I agree, but we need to stay alert. I'm not really comfortable leaving you three here alone while we are out exploring."

"I guess now is as good a time as ever to tell you that we have protection," Tim said. "I hid a gun in one of the equipment bags. I know I should have told you earlier, but I didn't want you to think I was just a scared little tech guy."

"I'm glad to hear that. I almost feel better knowing we have three weapons instead of just two," Bill said and smiled.

"Let's set Mr. Long's food outside in the box and call it a night. I'm thinking tomorrow will be a busy day," Mark said.

They placed the food in the box on the deck and closed the lid. The crew retreated to the bedroom, but not until Elaine watched Tim lock the door. She checked it herself to be sure it was securely locked.

\*\*\*

Back at the command center, Rob Hutchins was staring at the weather radar screen intensely. He was trying to figure out exactly what this unexpected weather front was going to do. The editing producer and the captain of the boat, who delivered everyone to the port, were also studying the monitor.

"Looks like a pretty big storm. How long do you think it's gonna last, Captain?" Rob asked.

"Probably be around for a day, maybe two. It's really hard to predict these things up here," the captain answered.

"Do you think we should tell the crew to be on the lookout for nasty weather or at least not to be caught out in it when exploring the area?" the editing producer asked.

"There can be some strong winds associated with storms like this, but the cabins should provide adequate protection," the captain replied.

"What about Mr. Long's quarters?" Rob asked.

The captain stopped staring at the monitor's screen and looked at Rob and asked, "Did you say it was an old hunting stand that had been remodeled by the construction crew?"

"Yeah, that's right," Rob said.

"Well, that hunting stand has survived many storms already, Rob. The remodel job would only make it stronger, right?" the captain said.

"Yes, we'll keep an eye on the storm, and I can call them tomorrow night to give them a heads up on the weather if the situation requires it," Rob replied.

***

Back at the hunting stand, Bob Long's alarm sounded at just about the same time the crew had entered their cabin after supper. He slowly rolled over in his sleeping bag, slid out his arms, and stretched as far as they could reach.

For a brief moment, Bob thought, *It sure would be nice to wake up in my own bed back in Montana.* He slowly climbed out of the sleeping bag and began to dress for the night's excursion.

He heated the water for his coffee on the portable stove that accompanied his small but cozy quarters. Bob opened the container that held his rations for the day, and it looked like breakfast, or whatever this meal was called, would be eggs and sausage. *Not a bad combination for a meal out in the middle of nowhere*, he thought.

Bob could clearly remember eating a lot worse on other trips he had endured. After finishing the food, he leaned back against the wall of the shelter, savoring the rest of his morning coffee. Different scenarios that he could inflict on the contestants ran through his mind. Every now and then, a smile would appear on Bob's face as he visualized what might go through the contestants' minds as he acted out the shenanigans in the darkness around their cabins.

After sipping the last drop of coffee, Bob readied himself for the ninety-minute hike to the others. He grabbed a pack of peanut butter crackers and his camelback full of water. He exited the stand, switched on his night vision goggles, and began to make his way to the old, abandoned road. Probably not a hundred yards from the stand, Bob encountered a smell. It was the same odor he had noticed the night before. He stopped and took the time to slowly survey the entire area around him through the goggles. Bob couldn't see anything, but he had the feeling he was being watched again. The forest was deadly silent; there was not a sound to be heard.

He checked to make sure his pistol was securely fastened to his side. The fact that it was there eased Bob's mind a little, but he still had an uneasy feeling in his gut. He maneuvered down through the trees and the small scrub bushes. He stopped every now and then to perform a quick scan, but nothing could be seen in the goggles. But the odor was still evident.

As he moved forward, Bob was trying to cypher what was going on around him. The odor wasn't getting any stronger or weaker. It was almost like the smell was merely following him. He stopped more frequently than the night before just to do several quick checks on the surroundings. He stared intently up the mountain when a twig, down the mountain, abruptly snapped and broke the silence in the forest.

Bob immediately turned to the direction of the sound. He had been stalked by animals before in the wild, but this felt strangely different...much different. He took a couple of steps when something suddenly came crashing down the mountain towards him. Bob instinctively unholstered his gun and turned to meet whatever was charging down the mountain. When he turned, he saw a rock the size of a softball bouncing in his direction at an alarming rate of speed.

Bob barely had time to retreat behind a large tree as the rock passed by and bounced down the mountain. He quickly came out from behind the tree and peered up the mountain. He couldn't see anything moving. He could only see the shape of trees and bushes, but he heard something. Something was moving below him. He heard it take a couple of steps at a time, and it stopped. It took a couple of steps and stopped again.

Bob tried to see the movement, but the area was too dense and thick below him. He slowly walked a little further out on the mountain before he turned down to the road. He made his way cautiously out on the side of the mountain in the direction of the sound. It was moving through the area just below him. Bob paused periodically to listen. He thought, *It's like being driven like an animal.* The movement paused at the same time he paused, but the odor didn't change. It hadn't changed since he first got wind of it outside the stand. He knew that last night the smell had only lasted for a small time, like a dead animal nearby. Tonight, the odor seemed to be following him wherever he went.

Bob whispered to himself, "Dead animals don't move through the woods."

Bob heard what he believed was a low grunt, and it was coming from behind him. He heard another low grunt from above him. He heard leaves rustle below him. Down on the hill below him, Bob knew something was moving. He could not see it clearly.

*What is that?* Bob thought as he struggled to see through the darkness. *Is it standing on two legs? Is it one of the contestants or crew? There's not supposed to be anyone else here at the port.*

Bob quietly took another step to identify what was standing there looking up at him. He totally focused on what was there, when he suddenly felt a warm breath of air on the back of his neck. In an instant, he realized that the notion of being driven like an animal was indeed what had just happened.

Bob reached for his weapon again and tried to turn around, but it was much too late. Two massive hands gripped his head and started to squeeze. The creature lifted Bob off the ground. Bob kicked his feet and legs and dropped his pistol. Bob violently pulled and tried to pry off the hands that gripped his head. It was no use. Bob knew that he wasn't going to see what had him. He couldn't see anything because the creature had knocked his goggles off when it grabbed him. He heard the rustle of the leaves below him, and whatever was there was charging up the mountainside to him.

Bob felt his body go limp. With the immense pressure applied to the sides of his head, everything was going dark. His legs stopped flailing around, and his arms and hands dropped. Bob was unconscious. With the creature's final squeeze, the creature crushed Bob's skull and ended his life.

The forest fell silent. The only sounds that could be heard were the heavy breathing noises coming from the three creatures that surrounded Bob's body, lying lifeless in the leaves.

\*\*\*

Back at the cabins, sleep didn't come easy for some of the crew. Andre tossed and turned several times in his sleeping bag. He kept running the days' events through his mind. He thought, *What had placed the stones on the deck railing, and just what did they mean? Did the smell belong to the "whatever," and did it put the stones there? What was really here at the port? Could this Hairy Man creature be real? Did the people, many years ago, encounter him? Were their drawings in the journals correct?*

His racing thoughts wouldn't allow him to sleep.

Elaine was beginning to question whether she had made the right decision to come here. She asked herself if the money to help with her student loans was really worth what she suddenly felt was imminent danger. She wondered if maybe it would've been to her advantage to spend more time with her father on some of his hunting excursions.

Mark pondered about the bones at the homestead. He kept asking himself, *What exactly had crushed the man's skull? Why were the bones scattered throughout the cabin? Had the door been kicked in, or did it just simply collapse inside of the cabin after years of being in the elements?* There were so many questions, and so few answers.

Dave Murrows suddenly awoke as if something moved beside the cabin. He thought, *Was that the wind? Did the wind just pick up?* He listened closely. The movement stopped. It started again. No, that's not the wind. That sounded as though a person was moving through the small bushes along the side of the cabin and stopping periodically to check the surroundings. He stopped breathing and listened intently. He heard a low grunt sound coming from outside the back corner of the room where they were all sleeping.

Dave slowly raised in his bunk and listened closely. He heard something sliding along the side of the cabin. It would stop and then start again. *There's something out there*, Dave thought.

It was nearly impossible to look out the window and see anything. They had opted to leave a lamp on ever since something had run across the deck. But if there was something outside, it would be really easy for it to look in on them. Dave wasn't very fond of that idea. He realized that easing out of his sleeping bag and turning off the lamp would alarm whatever was out there.

"You heard that, Dave?" Ronnie whispered.

"Yes," Dave whispered back toward Ronnie.

"It's been out there for several minutes. I think it's already been around the cabin once," Sasha said nervously.

"Let's move quietly to the front of the cabin. We might be able to see something out one of the windows with the lights off," Dave suggested.

The three of them quietly climbed out of their sleeping bags and headed to the kitchen area. Dave and Ronnie had just cleared the opening to the kitchen, and Sasha was right behind them beside the bathroom door when there was a loud thump on the side of the cabin.

Sasha could not stop herself. She let out a shriek, and either the thump or her shriek woke the remaining people in the cabin. Everyone listened. It sounded like something or someone slapping the cabin with a leaf covered branch. It was not one side of the cabin, but all around the cabin.

Ronnie silently made his way to the right-side window. He could still hear the slapping sound, but he was unable to see anything in the darkness of the night.

"Can you see anything, Ronnie?" Dave asked.

When Ronnie turned to answer, he saw a figure or a shadow go by the window behind Dave. "There, Dave. Something just ran by the window."

All three were staring at the window behind Dave when the branch slapped the window near where Ronnie was standing. Ronnie gasped.

There were two more thuds. After that, they could hear something running through the brush away from the cabins.

"What was that?" Sasha asked with fright.

"I'm not sure, but there was more than one. I don't believe it was a bear this time," Dave answered bravely.

From the bedroom, Willy yelled out, "Did you guys see anything from in there?"

"I saw something go by the window behind Dave. It looked like an upright figure, but it's so dark outside I can't say for sure," Ronnie said, and they walked back into the bedroom.

"I know we all agreed to sleep with this lamp on, but I don't like the fact that something can see in when we cannot see out," Dave said.

"I agree," Stan said. "If something is outside on the deck, there's no way you are going to see it from in here with the light on."

"If we need to turn it on, it's easy enough to do. I think we should leave it off, so nothing has a clear view of us," Dave said.

Reluctantly, they all agreed to turned off the light and climbed back into their sleeping bags. They called it a night.

# CHAPTER 9

Early the next morning, the crew climbed out of their bunks and began to meander through the cabin. Bill started to make the morning lift-me-up coffee, Mark and Tim were still sitting on the sides of their bunks, and Elaine was brushing her teeth. Andre just finished checking the equipment they had put on charge the night before. When he stood, he noticed the eight people next door were all outside surveying the deck and the cabin surroundings.

"Hey, Bill, take a look outside. Wonder what's going on next door?" Andre said.

Bill stepped back to look out the window. "Don't have a clue, but it sure appears that they're working hard after whatever they are looking for."

Mark and Tim walked into the room. Elaine sat down her toothbrush and followed right behind them.

"I don't know what they are looking for or at, but there's a lot of activity going on over there," Elaine claimed.

"Here's everybody's coffee. Now, let's go out on the deck and find out what's going on," Bill said.

The five of them ambled outside and, at first, none of the contestants noticed them standing there. All eight were absorbed in studying everything on the deck and beside the cabin. It reminded the crew of a bunch of ants scurrying around. There had to be a purpose in what they were doing, but it just didn't quite make sense to the crew.

Finally, Shelley looked up and asked, "Did you people hear anything last night?"

The crew glanced at each other with a puzzled look on their faces. They were sure that if something had happened, they surely would have heard it.

Sandy came around the corner of the cabin and announced, "Last night, something was on the deck again. It was beating against the side of the cabin with this limb." She pointed to the floor of the deck. There was a four-to-five-foot branch lying there.

"Dave, Ronnie, and Sasha all heard it moving through the bushes and—" Willy began, standing in the small scrub bushes between the cabins.

Stan interrupted and said, "Ronnie thinks he saw something move by the window on the other side of the cabin. Whatever visited last night, there were at least two of them. Maybe more."

"There is something that's kind of confusing, though," Shelley said.

"What's that, Shelley?" Mark asked.

"Did one of you set these rocks on the porch railing?" Shelley answered with another question.

Andre and Elaine stared at each other for a couple of seconds, but neither spoke.

"I assure you that we didn't place the stones on the railing. We were all sound asleep," Mark said, looking at Shelley.

"Well, they didn't put themselves there," Shelley said. "Someone or something set thirteen stones all in a row on that railing."

"I assure you people that we had nothing to do with them," Bill said firmly.

Tim looked at Andre, but Andre was focused directly on the stones lying on the railing next door. Andre thought, *Shelley said there were thirteen stones, but at supper last night, the number was fourteen. Had a stone been knocked off by a bird or something? Why had the number changed?*

The crew asked if they had found anything other than the limb or rocks from last night's activity. The contestants indicated that was all they had found. The crew walked over to the contestants' cabin and stood there on the deck until the other eight had assembled. One at a time, they walked through the door.

Andre, once again, was the last in line and before he entered the cabin. He paused briefly to count the stones again. Sure enough, there were only thirteen, and they were lying there completely undisturbed. After taking a long look around, he followed the others inside. Andre didn't realize that there were a pair of eyes on him taking a long look back at him.

The group fixed breakfast, and everyone either sat or stood to eat. The crew was amazed at the chattering of the contestants. For a bunch of people who had only met a couple of days ago, they acted like they had known each other for years. The same story was repeated over and over. The story about the sound in the brush, the limb slapping the side of the cabin, and the thud on the cabin walls.

Dave interrupted everyone's conversation. "Hey, guys, I just remembered. I also heard a low grunting sound coming from outside last night."

Andre wondered if this could be the same grunting sound he heard coming back to the cabin. Even Tim and Bill heard it. But Andre didn't say anything.

There were more questions directed to Dave. He did the best he could to describe and imitate the grunting noise.

After breakfast, Mark told the contestants to think about their plans for the day while they readied the equipment. The crew departed and headed next door. As soon as the door was closed, the conversation began. Andre was first to start the conversation.

"Now, I'm more confused about the pebbles than ever," he said. "First there was one, then two, next fourteen, now back to thirteen...What's up with the number of pebbles changing?"

"Do you think last night's grunting sound was the same as the one you heard?" Elaine asked.

"Can't say for sure, but all this does seem a little odd," Andre answered.

"Odd is an understatement, don't you think?" Elaine asked.

"I agree there has been a lot of strange things that we have encountered since we got here, but before we make idiots out of ourselves to Rob, let's make sure of our evidence and our facts," Mark said. "Mr. Long could have been responsible for last night. Maybe while he ran through the bushes on one side of cabin, he threw a rock to the other side. That would explain something moving on both sides."

"I agree, but remember, we've already decided yesterday that Bob couldn't have been in two places at once," Bill said. "And now, make that three places counting what took place here, with the odor and the stones. I think we all need to stay on our toes at all times. Keep a sharp eye out, and we need to concentrate more on our surroundings than the filming of the group."

Mark nodded in agreement, looked at Tim, and said, "Make sure you three stick together, and keep that weapon with you."

\*\*\*

Back at the command center, everyone was studying the storm on the weather radar screen.

"Looks like we might get lucky, people. I don't think she's gonna be as big a storm as we thought," Rob said.

The captain took a sip of coffee and said, "It does appear to be breaking apart somewhat. We'll need to keep an eye on her, though. She could regroup."

"I'm not going to say anything to the crew until we know for sure what the storm is going to do," Rob said. "There should be plenty of time to warn them if it gains strength and heads in their direction."

The director looked at the captain for his approval since he was the most informed individual in the room. The captain looked directly into the director's eyes and grinned slightly.

"We'll be able to figure out the storm in time to have everyone batten down the hatches if needed."

\*\*\*

Everyone assembled outside the crew's cabin to begin the day's excursion. Andre, Tim, and Elaine all leaned on the deck railing to the side of the steps, just observing the activity of the others.

"You guys came up with a plan for today?" Bill asked the contestants.

"We thought we would stay in the same groups as yesterday and go in the same directions," Dave said. "Our group wants to take another look around the homestead and the clearing. The other group wants to check the grassy meadow for more clues on what they saw moving to the tree line."

"Sounds like a plan. Let's get going," Bill said.

The three hanging back at the cabin watched as the two groups departed and disappeared from sight.

A chill suddenly came over Elaine. "I'm not sure we should get separated from each other," she said. "I feel like whatever was here seventy-five years ago still walks these woods."

Andre looked at Elaine and then turned to Tim. "You make sure you have that weapon handy at all times," he said.

"It's right here on my side," Tim assured. "Let's all stay focused and alert. But I wonder why Mr. Long hasn't called this morning to check on the group's activity for the day."

"That is kind of odd. Think he's sleeping in?" Andre asked.

"He called pretty early yesterday. Let's check the tracker and see where he is," Tim suggested.

Andre powered up the tracking device, and all three studied the screen. Elaine studied the screen too, even though she wasn't totally sure of what exactly she was looking at. Soon the tracker stabilized after acquiring GPS, and immediately Tim and Andre noticed something odd.

"Is that Bob?" Elaine asked and pointed to the dot on the screen.

"Yes, theoretically," Tim replied.

"What does that mean?" Elaine asked, picking up on Tim's uncertainty.

"If Bob still has the transmitter on him, he's nowhere near his cabin this morning," Andre responded.

"Then, where is he?" Elaine asked.

Andre glanced at Tim, and they both looked back at the screen.

"It looks like he's above the old, abandoned road leading to the homestead that Mark's group found yesterday," Andre said.

"Maybe he figured the group would be coming that way again this morning, and he's planning to intercept them on the way," Elaine said hopefully.

"I don't think so," Tim said. "He's a long way above the road. Should we call Mark on the walkie-talkie?"

Andre was still staring at the screen. "Maybe he dropped the transmitter either coming here or going back last night."

"Hey, guys, he called us on the SAT Phone," Elaine said. "Let's try to call him."

Andre walked to the nightstand beside the crew's equipment, picked up the Sat Phone, and called Mr. Long. All three waited patiently, expecting Bob to say hello at any second. There was no answer.

Mark's group made their way down the abandoned road to the homestead. They noticed nothing new other than their own footprints they made the day before. They finally broke through the trees and brush of the small meadow to the rundown homestead. They all just stood there for a couple of seconds, taking in the scenery.

Betty thought, *This appears so peaceful, but at some time, something very violent occurred here — something that cost someone their life.*

"Let's be real attentive, people," Willy broke the silence. "Look at every detail. We need to gather all the evidence we can."

The entire group acknowledged him with a nod and moved toward the homestead. They scoured the area. Mark seized the opportunity to film each of the contestants in their individual search for clues.

Dave entered the homestead through the same door as yesterday and looked at every item inside. He moved slowly through what had been the kitchen. He, again, observed the crushed skull lying on the floor. He wondered aloud about what could have caused the violence and the hole in the skull.

Suddenly, he heard a noise near the fireplace. He quickly turned in the direction of the noise. He was greeted with a small mouse as it exited behind a stack of wood. It scurried to an opening in the outside wall that a ray of sunlight was beaming through. After taking a deep breath and regaining his composure, he noticed that the ray of sunlight was shining on something of an odd shape. He slowly made his way to the object.

He recognized it even before he got over to it. Slightly protruding from beneath what appeared to be an old pillowcase, it was a human jawbone. Dave took what was left of a chair leg and removed the cloth covering the jawbone.

This meant that two people had lost their lives in this cabin. Dave searched more closely and quickly found the rest of the skull that the jawbone belonged to. He soon found several more bones that belonged to this second individual.

Dave wondered out loud, "What happened here?"

Willy was in the tool shed searching for answers. The tool shed appeared like it had not been disturbed in years. The tools looked eerie. It was like they had been placed in their rightful spot and never bothered again.

Sasha and Betty searched the field surrounding the homestead. They found nothing interesting except for the sheer number of paths through the grass and brush. They discussed what could be moving back and forth, and why so often. They just figured it was the animals that inhabited the area.

***

Back at the cabin, Tim checked the monitor for what seemed to be the tenth time. There was still no movement on Bob's transmitter. Once again, Andre called Bob on the SAT Phone, but still no answer.

"Maybe Bob has been injured and needs help. We need to do something," Elaine said.

"Let's call Mark on the walkie-talkie," Andre suggested. "They can leave the homestead and check on Bob on the way back."

***

Mark was filming Sasha and Betty when he heard the walkie-talkie come to life.

"Hey, Mark, this is Andre, can you hear me, buddy?"

Mark retrieved the unit from his side and replied, "Loud and clear, what's up?"

"How's it going there? You guys find anything?" Andre asked.

"Not sure yet," Mark answered. "I've been filming the group from a distance as they search."

"Are you still by yourself?" Andre asked.

Mark pushed the key button and replied, "Yeah, nobody can hear me if that's what you mean."

Andre responded, "We could have a problem. Bob Long's transmitter is not at his cabin, and it hasn't moved all day."

"Where does it show he's at?" Mark asked.

"Quite a ways above the abandoned road between here and there. Should the three of us check it out, or what?" Andre asked.

Mark started to speak when Andre interrupted him, saying, "We've tried to call him on the SAT Phone, but there's no answer. Something's not right, Mark."

"Then we don't want anyone to know about Bob just yet," Mark said. "Looks like there might be a little rain moving in. I think I can get the group to return a little early, and then one of you can go with me to check on Bob."

"Elaine wants us to check pretty quickly in case he needs medical attention," Andre said. "When you guys get back, you and I will go to the transmitter."

"Elaine can get an emergency kit together, and we'll leave as soon as we get back," Mark replied.

"Roger that," Andre said.

Andre released the key button, and Elaine said, "I think I should go with you guys."

"You sure about that, Elaine?" Tim asked.

"Taking care of the medical situations here is my responsibility," Elaine answered.

"We are not even sure if there is a situation yet," Tim added.

"True, but we're not sure there isn't one either," Elaine said.

Elaine turned and gathered the supplies she deemed necessary to take with her. Andre and Tim glanced at each other and eyed each other for a few seconds, but no words were spoken.

\*\*\*

Bill and the second group ambled in single file out into the grassy meadow at the head of the bay. All was calm, but it was an eerie calmness. A gentle breeze blowing made the tops of the tall grass move as though they were dancing to the sound of music. All of them made their way to the edge of the stream, where they had stood the day before, and surveyed the surrounding area. Something caught Shelley's attention.

Shelley looked at the tree line and thought, *What is that standing in the tree line? Is that a person? It is standing upright. It's looking in our direction.*

Shelley continued to stare at the figure. It seemed to melt into the brush and trees until she could no longer see it clearly. She questioned herself: *Did I really see something or was it just my imagination? Was this similar to what Betty had seen in the tree line above the remains of the old processing plant?*

"Ronnie, how about you and I check out more of the meadow?" Stan said, interrupting Shelley's thoughts. "Maybe there are more bedding areas like the one we found yesterday."

"Sounds good. What's your plan, gals?" Ronnie asked.

Sandy looked over at Shelley and asked, "How about we check the banks of the stream and see what we come up with?"

"Sounds good to me. There might be some footprints along the edge," Shelley said.

*** 

Bill took the opportunity to climb up on a large rock beside the stream so he could do some filming of the group. He thought to himself, *Maybe I should check in with the crew at the cabins.*

Bill retrieved the walkie-talkie from his pack, turned it on, and keyed the transmit button. "Hey, Tim, this is Bill. Do you read me?"

Back at the cabin, all three heard Bill's voice coming through loud and clear on their end.

Tim rushed over and grabbed the radio. "Yeah, Bill, got you loud and clear," Tim answered.

"Just wanted to check in," Bill said. "We are at the meadow, and the group is hunting for clues."

"No surprises yet?" Tim asked.

"Not yet, and I kind of hope there aren't any, either," Bill chuckled.

"Keep your eyes and ears open, Bill. Stay alert," Tim said.

Bill detected something wrong in Tim's voice. "Something I need to know about, Tim?"

"We're not sure...Can you talk?" Tim responded.

"Yeah, the others can't hear us," Bill replied.

"Well, we are not sure yet, but Mr. Long's transmitter is nowhere near his cabin, and it hasn't moved all day long," Tim explained. "He doesn't answer the SAT Phone either. Mark's group is going to come back a little early, and Mark and Andre are going to check it out."

"Should we call Rob?" Bill asked.

"Give them a chance to investigate, and then we'll have to make that decision," Tim said.

"Okay, we'll just keep snooping around up here. See you when we get back," Bill confirmed.

"Roger that," Tim said. "Be careful."

Bill clipped the walkie-talkie to the strap of his backpack and reassured himself of the weapon he was carrying. He grabbed the pistol grip and squeezed it tightly.

# CHAPTER 10

Everyone at the command center intently stared at the weather radar screen — all of them except the editing producer, who was pacing back and forth in the dimly lit room and keeping his eyes focused on the floor.

Rob finally looked up and said, "Man, will you please settle down? If this thing gets any stronger, it will happen during the night, and everyone will be safe in their cabins. They won't venture out till the weather breaks."

The producer stopped pacing and looked at the captain. "You agree?"

The captain nodded yes, but the editing producer still had an uneasy feeling about the storm and the safety of all at the port.

***

Dave emerged from the door of the homestead and said, "Hey, guys, I found something that you need to see."

Willy took one more look around the undisturbed shed and moved toward Dave, who seemed to be staring at nothing. Sasha, Betty, and Mark all made their way to the homestead.

Dave waited for the group to gather and announced, "There was more than one person killed in this cabin."

"How do you know that, Dave?" Willy asked.

Dave entered the door and stopped in the kitchen area. He pointed to his right. "Over next to the fireplace, there's another jawbone. There are more bones scattered around in that area too." After a small pause, he continued, "It looks like this person was also physically torn apart. I'm telling you people, something evil happened here."

The others walked slowly over to the fireplace. It didn't take long for them to realize that Dave had indeed discovered a second victim. He was right. The bones scattered around were not in any organized manner. They could have been moved by some small creature, but it looked like this person had been literally torn limb from limb.

"What kills two people, rips them limb from limb, and gets away without a hitch?" Betty asked hesitantly.

None of the group had an answer for Betty.

"These people had to be tough to live out here in the wilderness, to survive in this harsh environment, and then to die in this manner," Betty added.

Mark had a million things running through his mind. *Was this Hairy Man for real, and what really happened here at the homestead? What about Mr. Long? Why was his transmitter out in the middle of the woods? Why didn't he answer his SAT Phone? Had Mr. Long run into whatever had done this?*

There were so many questions without any answers. Mark wanted to tell the contestants about Mr. Long, so they could check on him on their way back, but at the same time he didn't want to jump the gun and possibly ruin the show. He knew that Rob would not be very happy about that.

Mark gathered his thoughts and then spoke to the group. "Andre called me on the walkie-talkie, and it looks like some rain is moving in. Let's get back and explain to the other group what all we have found. Maybe tomorrow, all of us can come back out here and see what their take on the situation is. If they come to the same conclusions as we have, then there may be more homesteads down this road to take a look at. We could go as one group and check them out, and that way, we might be able to get a clearer picture of what happened here."

All agreed, and they made their way to the road and headed back. The breeze had become a little stronger, and the clouds began to darken as they walked in single file up the old, abandoned road. All of them wondered what could have possibly happened at the homestead — all of them except Mark.

All Mark could think about was Bob Long.

At the meadow, Shelley and Sandy combed the banks of the stream. Stan moved through the grass to the tree line where something had disappeared the day before. Ronnie ventured down to the edge of the field where the grass met the shoreline. Bill was still perched atop the rock filming their progress.

Each member of the group suddenly stopped what they were doing, lifted their heads, and turned toward the mountainside behind them. The bellowing growl emerged from the distance, and it enhanced the chill that began to fill the air.

Stan had never heard anything like that before in his life. He was completely oblivious to his surroundings until the small twig behind him snapped. He spun around and faced a massive figure standing. He needed to scream. He needed to inhale a breath. He gasped as the creature grabbed him by the neck. It squeezed tightly as it pulled Stan down in the grass. Stan fought with all his strength, with arms flailing and kicking his feet feverishly. But he was no match for the sheer power of this creature. Stan's neck snapped and cracked. The blood stopped flowing to his brain. His neck simply collapsed, and the skin burst and erupted, gushing blood from Stan's neck.

At first, all remained perfectly quiet and still. All were frozen where they stood. Bill was the first to turn and look at the others. He looked at the terrified expressions on the girls' faces, then at Ronnie, and then in Stan's direction. Bill had looked at him just seconds before, and now, Stan was nowhere to be seen.

Without warning, there was another growl from the head of the meadow followed by several grunts. Shelley and Sandy immediately moved towards Bill. Ronnie remained frozen at the edge of the grass. The girls approached Bill and looked up at him on the rock. He moved his head as he surveyed the area.

"What was that?" Sandy whispered slowly.

"I'm not sure, but I don't think we are alone here," Bill quietly replied.

Bill glanced at Ronnie and with a simple hand gesture motioned for him to come back to them. Ronnie crouched over just enough to see over the grass and quickly made his way to the group. Bill peered in Stan's direction but didn't see him anywhere. He thought, *Did Stan hide in fear? Did he see something?*

"Where's Stan?" Shelley asked nervously.

"He was right there at the tree line, and after the first growl, I looked back and he was gone," Bill said, continuing to scan the meadow.

Ronnie approached the group and stood beside the girls. He moved in all directions as if he were expecting something to come at any moment.

"Do you see Stan?" Shelley asked again, cautiously.

Bill looked around in search of Stan. "I don't see anything, nothing at all."

"Can you see any grass moving? Maybe he's crawling back to us," Ronnie whispered.

"I don't see anything, people. I'm going to check on Stan," Bill said and removed the weapon from its holster.

"I think we should all go together. We only have one weapon, and we are stronger as a group," Ronnie said.

Bill glanced at the girls, then back to Stan's direction. "What do you think? Do we go as a group to check on Stan or not?"

"I agree with Ronnie," Shelley said. "We're better as a group, plus I don't want to be standing here without any protection."

"The last time I saw Stan, he was standing at the spot where whatever moved had disappeared through the grass yesterday," Bill said.

The four of them made their way through the meadow and looked and watched in all directions. They followed the path that Stan made when he moved through the grass. Suddenly, Sandy stopped and grabbed Shelley by the arm.

"What's the matter, Sandy?" Shelley whispered in panic.

"You guys smell that?" Sandy asked. "Sasha and I smelled the same thing coming up the trail to the cabins the second morning we were here."

All looked at each other as fear gripped them.

"Everybody, keep a sharp eye out and stay close," Bill said bravely.

Bill methodically placed one step in front of the other as he led the group. When they reached the edge of the woods, Bill gasped and fell to his knees.

There was Stan's limp body with a small trickle of blood still oozing from his neck. His eyes were wide open and appeared to be ready to pop out of their sockets.

Shelley and Sandy saw Stan's body at the same time. Their facial expressions turned to horror and disbelief. Ronnie bumped into Sandy as he cautiously kept an eye out behind the group. He turned and saw Stan. Nobody spoke. Nobody moved. It was as if time stood still.

Bill, still on his knees, turned and looked at the others. "We've got to get back to the cabins," he said, controlling his emotions.

"We have to take Stan back with us," Shelley said quietly.

"Don't you realize that whatever did this to Stan and made those noises is probably still watching us?" Bill asked sternly.

"Bill's right," Sandy said coldly. "There's nothing we can do for Stan. We need to get back as fast as we can."

"I'm not leaving Stan. I'll carry him back myself," Ronnie said firmly.

Everyone was silent for a moment.

"I agree with Ronnie," Shelley said. "I'll help with Stan. You two do whatever your heart tells you to do."

Bill stared at Shelley in disbelief. "Listen, I don't like the idea of leaving Stan either. But whatever creature did this, it's a powerful animal. I think we should all go back together, get the others, and come back for Stan."

"We're not leaving Stan here!" Shelley snapped. "No telling what animal may come along and...possibly drag him away."

Everyone knew that the thought of *Stan's body* being dragged off was not what was running through Shelley's mind, but nobody dared to correct her.

"You two start back," Ronnie said. "Get to the cabins as quickly as you can and get some help. Shelley and I will start working our way back down the road with Stan. Don't waste any time coming back."

Bill and Sandy looked at the others and nodded. They made their way through the grass towards the rock. Ronnie removed his jacket and wrapped it around Stan. With Shelley's help, he hoisted Stan over his shoulder.

Stan's Go-Pro camera that was around his neck fell to the ground. Shelley picked it up and put it around her neck.

"Do you think he got footage of the thing that did this to him?" Ronnie asked calmly.

"I don't know, but we'll take it back and see when we get to the cabins," Shelley said.

Shelley moved around Ronnie and looked him directly in the eyes and said, "We'll make our way slowly and methodically back to the road. I'll do my best to keep an eye out for anything and everything. Just don't overdo it. I don't want to be left out here alone."

"You got it," Ronnie replied. "I know this was the right thing to do, Shelley. I'm just not real fond of being out here without a weapon. It reminds me of being on that mountain in North Carolina."

\*\*\*

A fine mist began to fill the air as Mark and the members of group one reached the cabins. Mark was halfway up the steps to the crew's cabin when he turned toward the contestants and told them they would discuss the findings at the homestead with the others when they got back. He wanted to see what they thought of the findings. All agreed to the idea. They scurried to their cabin to escape the rain. Mark reached the cabin door and turned the knob, but it didn't move. He heard someone approaching the door, heard a click, and the door opened.

"Sorry, Mark. Just not taking any chances," Elaine apologized.

"Where's Tim and Andre?" Mark asked.

Elaine pointed across the room and answered, "They're at the table checking the monitor again."

Elaine stepped aside and Mark entered the cabin. She shut the door and proceeded to lock it. Mark glanced back at Elaine, gave her a small smile, but he noticed the concern on her face.

"Elaine, let's make sure of all the facts before jumping to conclusions," Mark said. "I haven't said anything to the members of the group. I didn't want to raise any suspicions. Andre and I will go and check out the transmitter; you and Tim stay here. If the others question why we left, tell them I've lost the walkie-talkie and we're going to go look for it."

"What if Mr. Long is injured?" Elaine asked.

"If he is, then we will attend to him out there, I assure you," Mark answered. "If we need your expertise, we'll call you on the walkie-talkie."

"Okay. I've gathered a simple first aid kit for you guys to take with you, but you've got to promise to call if you need me there," Elaine insisted.

"I promise, Elaine," Mark said and smiled.

Andre looked up and said, "Hey, Mark, take a look at this monitor. This locator dot has not moved all day. We tried him on the SAT Phone again, just a couple of minutes before Elaine let you in, but still no answer."

Mark stared at the screen. "Looks like it's about halfway down the old road, but quite a ways up the side of the hill. We should be able to get there, assess the situation, and get back before dark. Are you okay with going with me, Andre?"

"Yes, just make sure you got that weapon on you," Andre replied. "I got a bad feeling about this, Mark."

Mark glanced at Tim and said, "Let's make sure of what is going on before we call Rob at the command center. How are we exactly going to find this transmitter when we get down there?"

"The two of you can take the monitor with you, and it will lead you right to it," Tim answered.

Mark looked at Elaine and Tim and said, "Sounds like a plan. We'll keep in touch with the walkie-talkie."

Andre and Mark put on some rain gear, grabbed the monitor, and headed for the door.

Mark looked out the window at the contestants' cabin. He didn't see anyone, so hopefully nobody would even know that they were gone. They exited the door of the cabin and scurried down the steps. Soon, they were on the old, abandoned road. Tim and Elaine were the only ones to be suspicious of the activities.

# CHAPTER 11

At the command center, everyone was busy either looking at the weather monitor or reading each update of the storm as it came off the printer. Of course, the editing producer was still pacing back and forth through the room, and now he carried one of the updates rolled up in his hand.

"We need to call the crew and tell them about the storm," the editing producer finally said.

The captain, whose eyes were still glued to the screen, agreed. "I think he's right, Rob. It shouldn't be a problem for everyone to weather out the storm in the cabins. However, I wouldn't want anyone to be out in this. I think by early tomorrow afternoon, it will pass, and we'll be in good shape."

"I'll phone the crew and Mr. Long," Rob volunteered.

Rob dialed up the crew's SAT Phone, and when it rang, Tim and Elaine looked at each other. Tim rushed over and picked up the phone.

"Hello," Tim said.

"Who is this?" Rob asked.

"Tim," Tim answered.

"Hey, Tim, there's a pretty good storm moving in tonight a little after dark, and it should hang around through the morning, but it'll start clearing in the afternoon," Rob explained. "Shouldn't be a big problem, but just tell everyone to hang out in the cabins till it passes, okay?"

"Will do, boss. How big of a storm?" Tim asked.

"There could be periods of some heavy rain, lightning, and possibly some strong wind gusts from time to time," Rob said. "Anybody found anything interesting yet? Maybe a paranormal creature?"

Tim didn't find the question very amusing considering all that had transpired. He wanted to inform Rob about Mr. Long, but Mark had instructed not to disclose anything until they had more facts. Tim and Elaine stared at each other. Tim could tell that Elaine wanted him to spill the beans about Mr. Long, but he held back.

"They have split into two groups to search the area," Tim said. "They have found some interesting things. We all have some good film footage so far, and I think the show is gonna be a big success."

"Fantastic!" Rob exclaimed. "You guys eat a good supper and stay safe in the cabins till the storm passes. I will check back in after the storm."

Tim was halfway through a goodbye when he heard the phone click and go silent. Tim just shook his head in disgust.

"Great. Now we got a storm coming too," Elaine said with disappointment.

Tim sat the phone down and said, "Yeah, sure looks that way."

Back at the command center, Rob dialed Mr. Long and there was no answer. He took another look at the storm on the weather radar. After a small pause, he tried again with the same results. Rob glanced at the phone and sat it down.

"What's wrong?" the editing producer asked.

"Mr. Long isn't answering. He's probably still sleeping in after last night's excursion. He's an experienced outdoorsman and survivalist, but he won't take any chances in bad weather."

\*\*\*

After several minutes, Bill and Sandy finally reached the small but steep incline at the road. Bill paused before he continued. He scanned the entire area, looking in all directions. Sandy stood perfectly still, only moving her eyes from left to right, scanning the area around her. Nothing was moving. There weren't even any birds chirping or darting from tree to tree. The silence was deafening, and an eerie calm had come over the meadow and its surroundings. Bill turned slightly, looked at Sandy, and nodded for them to continue.

Sandy grabbed Bill's arm. "Something's wrong, Bill. It's too quiet."

Bill knew she was right. "Yeah, let's go. We got to get help."

"Maybe we shouldn't leave Ronnie and Shelley," Sandy said.

"We need to get back as quickly as we can. Unfortunately, I think they let their hearts overrule good judgment. They made their decision and that's that. Let's get to moving."

They climbed up the small incline on the bank and began to move down the road. Both could feel that something just wasn't right. Suddenly, Bill stopped and knelt on one knee. Sandy dropped down on both knees behind him.

"What is it, Bill?" Sandy asked in a whisper.

Bill reached for the walkie-talkie and said, "I almost forgot we had this thing."

He fumbled around, feeling the strap on the backpack and the case that held the radio. He grabbed it. But the unit was not in the case. Somewhere between the rock and Stan, or somewhere between Stan and where they were now, he had dropped the walkie-talkie.

"I've lost the radio," Bill sighed.

"Should we go back?" Sandy asked.

"No. Let's keep moving. We'll try to find it tomorrow with the help of the others."

Bill and Sandy came to their feet and started down the road once more.

Neither of them had a flashlight, and with the thickening of the dark clouds, the visibility down the old, abandoned road was getting worse and worse.

\*\*\*

Mark and Andre moved swiftly down the road toward the homestead, only to pause briefly to check the monitor. The slight mist in the air wasn't impeding their progress at all. They closed in on the point that they needed to turn and head up the mountain. Mark stopped and checked the monitor.

Mark glanced at the screen and looked up the mountain. "This looks like where we need to start up," he said reluctantly.

Andre peered at the monitor once more, and then looked up and faced the hillside. "Yeah, it's straight up the mountain. It's going to be a pretty good climb," Andre said.

"Let's check in with Tim," Mark suggested. He retrieved the walkie-talkie from its case on the backpack's strap and said, "Hey, Tim, you read us, buddy?"

Tim and Elaine each jumped a little from the sound coming through the radio. They exchanged a look and raced to the radio.

Tim picked up the radio and keyed the device. "Loud and clear, Mark."

"We are at the point to start up the mountain, and according to the monitor, Mr. Long's transmitter is straight up the mountain in front of us," Mark explained. "It's going to a pretty tough climb, though. It's probably going to take us a little while, okay?"

"Roger that," Tim said. "By the way, Rob called and informed us that there is a pretty good-sized storm moving in tonight. He said that there might be some heavy rain and possibly some strong wind gusts. Make sure you guys get back before it moves in."

"Will do," Mark replied. "You didn't mention anything about this situation, did you?"

"No, I kept our little secret intact. What if he tried to call Mr. Long?"

"I don't know, but we know he's not going to answer," Mark said. "We can address that later if we need to. Andre and I are going to start up the mountain. I'll call when we get to the transmitter."

"Roger, be careful." Tim ended the call.

Elaine had slowly moved to the window to look at the contestants' cabin during the conversation on the radios. She watched aimlessly for any activity among the group. They appeared to mainly be sitting around and talking. Dave added wood to the fire while everyone sipped on a cup of coffee to warm them. For reasons she was unsure of, Elaine focused on the deck railing. The mysterious stones were all sitting in a row. She began to count them. *That can't be right,* she thought. She silently counted them two more times.

"Tim, come over here," Elaine said and motioned for Tim to walk over to the window.

"What is it?" Tim asked.

"Get over here and look at the stones," Elaine said sternly.

Tim walked over to the window and looked directly at the rocks. "Yep, there they are...sitting in a row on the railing."

"Count them," Elaine said with irritation.

Time counted the rocks three times. Each count came to twelve. The thirteenth stone was gone. He scanned the deck and the ground below the railing. He turned to Elaine and said, "I only count twelve. There were thirteen before."

"Yes, in the beginning there were fourteen. Then the number became thirteen, and now it's just twelve," Elaine explained.

Tim sensed urgency in Elaine's voice. "Maybe something just knocked it off, Elaine. It could have been a bird or a chipmunk, or anything could have knocked it off the railing."

"Maybe, but something put those rocks there in the first place, and now it seems like something is removing them one at a time," Elaine said. "This is really weird, Tim. Maybe the stories about this place are true." She looked at Tim for a reaction.

Tim raised his eyebrows and said, "I'll admit it's strange, but let's keep our heads screwed on straight until we find out for sure. We don't need to spook ourselves out here, okay?"

Elaine just nodded as she glanced out the window one more time. She moved over to the fireplace to warm herself against the chill that had swept over her body.

If Elaine and Tim or one of the contestants had stepped outside, someone might have heard the grunts. They might have heard the odd chattering sounds from the side of the mountain. They might have heard the strange chattering sounds from the small hill behind the cabins. They might have smelled the musky odor that surrounded the cabins.

If someone had just glanced out a window, they might have seen the stone taken. But no one had stepped outside. So, Tim and Elaine were left wondering about the stones and their significance.

*** 

Bill suddenly stopped and asked, "Did you see that?"

"No. There's so little light in here I can barely see anything," Sandy replied quietly.

"I think something crossed the road," Bill said slowly.

Sandy peered over Bill's shoulder and asked, "What was it?"

"I'm not sure, but it almost appeared like a person or something walking on two legs. I think my eyes are starting to play tricks on me, Sandy."

There was a moment of silence. Both stared down the road, but neither could make out anything. No matter how hard they strained their eyes, they saw nothing.

Bill removed his pistol from its holster and said, "Come on, Sandy."

They moved forward and walked no more than ten steps when something came crashing through the trees above them. Bill immediately swung around and raised his head to look in the direction of the noise. A large rock struck Bill directly on the forehead, driving him to the ground.

Sandy heard something running through the brush and trees toward them, and another figure was coming down the road behind them. She reached out to Bill.

"Run! Run, Sandy!" Bill shouted.

In the blink of an eye, Sandy did not hesitate. She turned and ran down the road toward the cabins. Like an Olympic sprinter clearing the blocks, she was at full speed in just a few steps.

Bill, still on his hands and knees, tried desperately to locate the pistol. He heard the creatures closing in on him. Bill found the barrel of the gun and squeezed his hand around it when he felt something grab his backpack. In an instant, Bill was lifted completely off the ground.

For a brief moment, he made eye contact with the creature that had crossed the road in front of them. Suddenly, Bill went crashing through the brush. A thousand things ran through Bill's mind, but one thought overshadowed all others: *This thing is real.*

The massive creature grabbed Bill again and swung him around like a toy. It hurled Bill into the upper bank of the road. The fall knocked the wind completely out of him, and Bill gasped for air. He realized that he was tightly holding onto his pistol.

He turned the pistol and planted his hand firmly on the grip and shook as his finger came in contact with the trigger. Bill frantically moved the pistol in search of a target. For an instance, there was complete silence. The brief moment of silence was broken when, suddenly, two mighty muscular arms wrapped around Bill's chest and tightened around him.

Bill tried to fight and free his hand with the gun, but he was no match for the power of this thing. Bill managed to fire the gun once. The shot shattered the silence in the woods, but the bullet only buried harmlessly into the dirt of the old, abandoned road.

The last thought that ran through Bill's mind was how he felt the warm air on the back of his neck and how the musky odor penetrated his nostrils. Bill's sternum and ribcage finally gave way under the creature's squeeze, with fragments of bones piercing his heart and lungs. The creatures began to play a game of tug of war with Bill's body. His arms and legs, one by one, were torn from their sockets and tossed down the hillside. As his body parts scattered on the hillside, there were two large howls, and the creatures disappeared back into the trees and the darkness of the forest.

Sandy heard the gunshot but didn't dare slow down. She had only one thing on her mind and that was to get back to the cabins. She felt her heart pounding as she ran down the dimly lit corridor between the trees. Her heart was pounding from the fear and the adrenalin driving her every step. After running for what seemed like forever, she realized that she could smell the smoke coming from the chimneys of the cabins.

*I must be getting close*, she thought. She rounded a small bend in the road, and the dimly lit corridor gave way to some small scrub bushes and an occasional large pine tree. *Finally*, she thought, *I can see the cabins*. The cabins just below her came into view. Sandy slowed and came to a stop. She bent over and placed her hands on her knees. She sucked in the damp air as quickly as it was possible for a human to do. *Only a few more breaths, and I can finish this race.*

The silence of the port was broken once again when the loud howl was bellowed out from the mountain behind her. There was another howl in the distance beyond the first. Both of the sounds aimlessly echoed throughout the port behind her. Then, there was a third howl from beyond the cabins.

After a small pause, Sandy heard a series of grunts and some form of chattering coming from the area between her and the cabins. She suddenly realized that there were more of these creatures than just the two that rushed her and Bill. She wondered if Bill had shot one of the creatures. She wondered if Bill had escaped them and was now running down the road towards her.

*Should I wait for Bill, or should I continue to the cabins?* Sandy decided that her safety was at the cabins, and that seemed to be her only hope.

The area around the port fell silent again. There were no howls or grunts and not even a bird chirping. Sandy realized the only sound she could clearly hear was the beating of her heart and her gasping for air to replenish her body.

\*\*\*

The sound of the gunshot that tore through the late afternoon air at the meadow startled both Shelley and Ronnie. Shelley immediately fell to her knees in the tall grass. Ronnie slowly mimicked the gesture as he supported Stan's limp body on his shoulder. For a few seconds, neither of them moved and listened to the sounds of the meadow. They only heard the water of the stream rushing over the rocks.

Shelley never made eye contact with Ronnie and scanned the grass. "Oh, no, Ronnie," she said. "Something's happened. Bill would only fire the weapon if it was an emergency."

"I agree, Shelley. They've run into some kind of trouble. We can only hope that whatever they encountered, they were able to get past it."

Another howl came from the same spot where the gunshot had rung out at the old road. A second howl emerged from the hillside on the opposite side of the meadow. Both howls gently echoed through the hills and hollows that surrounded the meadow.

"Ronnie, these things are hunting us down one or two people at a time," Shelley said in a panic. "I'm not sure that we're going to make it back to the cabins."

"Shelley, I'm just as fearful as you," Ronnie said slowly. "I'm trembling all over. But right now, we have to remain as levelheaded as possible. If we don't, you might be right. I don't think we can travel the old road. We need to find an alternate route."

Shelley tried to re-focus on survival and said, "What about the shoreline of the bay? I know we ain't been down through there, and I don't know how difficult it will be, but I do know that I don't want to go back the way we came."

Ronnie nodded his head in agreement and said, "Sounds like a plan. We'll just take our time and work our way down the shore. If something goes wrong, Shelley, only worry about yourself."

"Let's get a move on," Shelley said.

Shelley raised to her feet, helped Ronnie stand, and glanced at Stan. It did cross her mind that she and Ronnie could meet the same fate as Stan. But for now, they were very much alive and needed to start moving. Together, they slowly inched towards the stream, constantly looking and listening for movement around them. There was nothing to be seen.

Once at the stream's edge, Shelley stopped and turned to Ronnie. She asked, "Think we just follow the stream down?"

"Yeah, let's follow the bank of the stream right to the shoreline," Ronnie said. "Just watch your step."

Shelley took a deep breath and began to traverse down the bank. Neither of them had any idea that standing behind a large tree at the lower side of the road were a large pair of dark eyes watching their every step as they moved along the bank.

# CHAPTER 12

It had been fifteen minutes since Mark and Andre left the road and began the journey up the mountainside. It was steeper, and the terrain was much rougher than the men had imagined it would be. Occasionally they had to use small saplings to assist them in making forward progress up the hill. Mark stopped and leaned back against a large tree to catch his breath and rest for a minute. Andre slid down against a small sapling and laid back on the ground, looking up at the thick canopy of the forest.

After a moment, Andre spoke, "I think this may take a little longer than we thought, Mark. This is pretty treacherous."

"I believe you may be correct, buddy," Mark replied. "But up ahead it appears to open up a bit. It doesn't look as steep either. Hopefully it will be a little easier climbing, maybe not as thick as what we've already endured."

"Boy, I hope so," Andre said. "Have we still got the transmitter on the monitor?"

Mark retrieved the locator from his pack and powered it up. He knelt down so Andre could look at the screen also. Both waited for the device to acquire satellites for GPS. Then, right on the screen, the bright yellow dot for the transmitter appeared.

Mark pointed at it and said, "Still there, directly in front of us. We're probably a third of the way up the mountain to it."

Andre looked up. "Well, let's go a little farther and see if we can get to the easier walking terrain you promised," he said.

"I don't remember promising anything," Mark said, smiling.

Both men stood, and Mark shut down the locator. He placed it back in the pack, and they started to climb again. Another twenty minutes of rough climbing, and they emerged from the thick underbrush in the forest to the spot Mark saw earlier. It did indeed open up somewhat, and to both men's pleasure, it wasn't nearly as steep as the incline they had just traversed. This time, the men could sit down comfortably without worrying about sliding back downhill and losing ground on what they had just achieved. Neither one liked the idea of having to climb even one inch of the mountainside below them again.

At first, both men sat quietly in the leaves, slowly scanning the forest for any activity. Secretly, both hoped that they observed nothing odd. There were droplets of rainwater falling all around them, gently impacting the ground where they rested. It was still — just a fine mist in the air. The droplets were from the water that gathered on the canopy leaves and grouped together to roll off the leaves and plummet to the forest floor. Both men's breathing had slowed enough for them to start conversing again.

Andre spoke first. "Mark..."

"What's on your mind?" Mark asked.

Andre answered his question with another question. "You think this thing could be real?"

Mark looked directly at Andre and replied, "I'm not sure. We saw some really strange things down at the homestead. If those people died from natural causes, then why were they not properly buried? I mean, dude, you should have seen how their bones were scattered about. It was like they were torn limb from limb. I just don't understand. I've never seen anything like it."

Andre dropped his head and looked at the leaves. "I'm telling you, man,

I don't like this place," he said. "Something doesn't feel right."

"I feel the same way," Mark agreed. He looked up the mountain before continuing, "Let's get a move on and see what's up there and get back to the cabins before dark. Getting caught out here after nightfall is not necessarily on my bucket list."

Andre simply nodded, and both men stood slowly. They placed one foot in front of the other and continued up the mountain. Even though the severity of the climb had indeed lessened, Andre could still feel the burning sensation in his thighs. After a few minutes, Mark stopped, removed the locator, and pressed the power button.

After the unit acquired satellites, the transmitter's location lit up on the screen. It was close now — dead ahead, just a little to the right. This time, Mark left the monitor on as they closed in on the transmitter.

***

Meanwhile, Shelley and Ronnie had slowly but methodically made their way down the bank of the stream, and now they were standing at the edge of the bay. Shelley thought to herself as she looked out over the water, *If it weren't for everything that occurred today, this would be a view that just about anybody would love to see.*

But Stan was dead. Shelley wasn't sure about Bill and Sandy, and there was no doubt that something evil lived here.

Ronnie nudged Shelley with his free hand.

"We've got to keep moving, Shelley," he said. "We have plenty of bank to walk on since the tide is out. We're not sure how long it is till high tide. The water may come up all the way to the tree line."

Shelley didn't even respond back. She slowly dropped off the bank, waded across the stream, and began to maneuver around the rocks and countless pieces of driftwood that littered the shoreline. Ronnie followed in Shelley's footsteps, only concentrating on his balance and making sure Stan was secure on his shoulder. They had passed the last of the grass of the meadow and were now walking halfway between the water and the tree line as they made their way toward the cabins. Shelley would periodically hear something moving above them. Ronnie heard it also. It was as though something was flanking them as they traveled down the shoreline.

Finally, Shelley stopped to ask, "You hear that, Ronnie?"

"Oh, yeah, I hear it," Ronnie said. "Just don't look up in the woods, Shelley. Keep focused ahead."

"It's hard not to look," Shelley replied.

"I know, but we don't want to make eye contact with whatever it is," Ronnie said. "We don't want to be perceived as a threat. Just keep looking forward. It could have already taken us down, but for some reason, it's merely shadowing us down the shoreline."

Shelley took a deep breath and started down the shoreline again, and Ronnie fell in line right behind her. But whatever was up in the woods kept pace with them as they walked. Neither Shelley nor Ronnie even dared to glance up into the woods and instead looked either straight ahead or straight down to navigate through the rocks and driftwood.

\*\*\*

Sandy had recuperated enough, she thought, to make her final sprint to the cabins in the distance. She knew there was something between her and her final destination, but it was now or never.

Sandy jumped into action and once again began to sprint toward the cabins. With every step, she could feel the adrenaline kicking in, so faster and faster she ran. With each little curve in the road Sandy could feel a little rush of satisfaction. *I'm going to make it*, she thought to herself.

Only a few more advances and a few more curves, and then she could bolt up the steps and burst through the door of the cabin. Sandy glanced down for a split second to check her footing, and when she raised her head, there it was. No time to duck or even raise her hands.

The large stick looked like a baseball bat swinging directly at her face. A glancing blow connected with the top right of Sandy's forehead. It didn't render Sandy unconscious, but it was forceful enough to knock her off her feet and to the side of the road.

Sandy, being the athletic type, wasn't giving up so easily. She remembered how quickly the creatures closed in on her and Bill. Realizing the object had been swung from the lower side of the road, Sandy turned and climbed the bank on all fours, then tore through the brush as fast as she could. She could hear the pounding of the footsteps behind her, but for now, Sandy held her own. She had to put some distance between herself and whatever was chasing her.

Sandy realized that she was no longer heading to the cabins, but instead was running away from them to the hill that overlooked them. She suddenly made a left turn with the precision of a cheetah chasing its prey and began to sprint down the hill. Just as she broke into a small, grassy area, something blindsided Sandy with the force of a professional linebacker of the NFL. She rolled twice in the knee-high grass, coming directly back to her feet. Then, Sandy heard two small grunts between her and the safety of the cabins.

Sandy stood there, frozen from fear and her concession to the fact that for the first time in a long time, she would not finish a race. In the next second, a massive hand impacted Sandy's head from behind, a rush of pain replaced the adrenalin, and she fell face first to the ground. She was barely conscious when the two creatures from below approached and knelt down in front of her. She could feel warm air as one of them leaned down and smelled Sandy's hair. Then, without warning, the large foot of the Hairy Man that had blindsided her came crashing down on Sandy's back. Her spine was crushed with the force of the blow, and the air spewed from her lungs.

Sandy's race was over.

\*\*\*

The minutes were passing like hours in the crew's cabin.

Tim was sitting at the table, staring at the walkie-talkie and waiting on Mark's voice to call out to him and Elaine. Elaine had made some fresh coffee, and she was sitting close to the fire in a chair she had slid next to the hearth to keep warm.

Elaine would glance at the fire, then at the floor, then repeat the gesture over and over. She was kind of thankful that Mark had made her stay at the cabin. At least she was warm and dry. Her mind was wandering in a million directions as she watched the flames dance between and over the logs. Were Mark and Andre okay? Exactly where was Mr. Long, and why didn't he answer the SAT Phone earlier? What about the other team?

Then, it dawned on her that the other team hadn't come back. Surely, they started back this way after the mist began to fill the air. Maybe they were on their way, maybe they just hadn't got to the cabins yet, or maybe they needed to be radioed.

Elaine turned in her chair and said, "We haven't heard from the other team, Tim. Should we holler at them on the radio?"

Tim continued staring. "They are probably on their way back," he said. "They should be here shortly."

"What if they ran into some trouble?" Elaine asked.

Tim's eyes left the radio and turned to Elaine. "Surely if they did, one of them would have radioed us," he said. "Plus, they do have a weapon, Elaine."

Elaine paused for a second and said sternly, "Don't you think Mr. Long was carrying a weapon? Now we're hunting for him."

Tim dropped his eyes back to the radio and glanced at the pistol beside it.

"Let's give it a few more minutes, okay?" he said. "Maybe Mark will holler back at us, and then we'll radio the other group if they're not back."

\*\*\*

After maneuvering for several minutes around the trees and obstacles as they climbed the mountainside, Mark came to a stop. He studied the forest floor for a couple of seconds. Finally, he looked at Andre.

"Okay, according to the monitor, we are right on top of the transmitter," Mark said. "Let's find this thing."

Andre removed a flashlight from his raincoat, turned it on, and began to search the ground around them. The men searched the leaves, beside the fallen logs, and around the gigantic trees that made up the mountainside forest. Neither man was having much luck, then suddenly, Mark lost his footing and fell, sliding up against a large, fallen tree.

As he struggled to stand once again, Mark grasped a limb of the downed tree and pulled himself up. Halfway standing, Mark caught sight of exactly what he was hoping not to find. There was Mr. Long, or so he assumed since he had never really met the guy. Mark couldn't believe what he was looking at.

Mark muttered in a low voice, "Andre, over here."

Andre turned to Mark, "You find the transmitter?"

"Yeah..." Mark trailed off. "And I believe we found Mr. Long."

"What's that?" Andre said.

Andre slowly walked over and stood beside Mark. He scanned the body with his flashlight. When the light settled on the head of the body, Andre wheeled around and dropped to his hands and knees. He didn't actually vomit, even though he wanted to. He gasped for air, his whole body trembling. It took several minutes for Andre to regain his composure.

All the while, Mark was studying the injury to Mr. Long's skull. There didn't seem to be any more injuries to the body.

Mark turned to Andre and said, "Mr. Long didn't fall. Something crushed his skull from both sides. Something squeezed from both sides like being put in a vise and tightened."

Andre raised up to his knees and placed his hands on his thighs. "What in the world could do this? And why not...consume what it killed?"

Mark, still studying Mr. Long, replied, "I'm not sure, but I don't think this is about obtaining food. I think it's more about territory, protecting what's yours, defending your home."

Andre was now feverishly scanning the forest. "So, you think this Hairy Man is for real?"

"I think these people left this port in a real big hurry, and some of them had some gruesome stories of the events that took place here," Mark said. "Mr. Long's skull is similar to what we found at the homestead. His body is still intact, though, but the injury to his head...Well, let's just say I've seen that injury before."

Mark dropped the backpack and unclipped the walkie-talkie. He pressed the transmit button.

"Tim, this is Mark. Come in, Tim."

\*\*\*

Back at the crew's cabin, Tim and Elaine both jumped to their feet at the sound of the walkie-talkie. Tim grabbed it.

"Go ahead, Mark," Tim said.

"Tim, we found the transmitter," said Mark. "And, Tim...I think we may be in trouble here."

Elaine reached over and gripped Tim's elbow. "Mr. Long?"

"What about Mr. Long?" Tim asked Mark.

"Mr. Long is dead," Mark replied through the walkie-talkie. "Listen, Tim. His injury is very similar to what our group discovered at the homestead."

"You need help out there?" Tim asked.

"No, I don't think there's anyway Andre and I can get Mr. Long's body back down to the abandoned road before dark," Mark replied. "This is pretty rough terrain, Tim. I'm going to cover him with my jacket, and we are going to start back. How about the other group, are they back yet?"

Tim replied, "No, not yet."

"Call them on the radio and tell them to return to the cabins, but don't say anything about Mr. Long," Mark said. "Then call Rob on the SAT Phone and inform him of everything."

"Roger that, Mark," Tim said. "You two hurry back here."

"Will do," Mark's voice said. "Out."

Tim switched the walkie-talkie from channel one to channel two.

"Hey, Bill, this is Tim," he said. "Do you read me?"

Tim and Elaine waited, but there was no reply.

"Bill, this is Tim, can you hear me, buddy?" he tried again.

Tim looked at Elaine and said, "Maybe they got the radio switched off. Let's call Rob."

The walkie-talkie was on, and it clearly received the transmission from Tim. Even though it sounded off in the grass of the meadow where it had been dropped, there was nobody there to hear Tim's words.

Elaine walked hurriedly to the bedroom of the cabin, picked up the SAT Phone, and brought it to Tim. He powered up the phone. Tim kept staring at the screen of the expensive piece of technology, then he shook his head.

"What's wrong?" Elaine asked.

Tim replied, still staring at the phone, "The phone's not picking up any satellites. These things are notorious for not acquiring signal in bad weather. Now even the storm is working against us."

"What do we do now?" Elaine asked.

"We wait...wait for the other group, wait for Mark and Andre, wait for the phone to pick up satellites. We just wait, Elaine."

Elaine walked back to the chair at the fireplace and sat down. Tim sat at the table and stared at the phone. Both were wondering about the others, who were not safely inside the cabins.

Each of them questioned whether they were even safe inside their own cabin.

# CHAPTER 13

In the contestants' cabin, the four members of group one were sitting around the fireplace, sipping on the coffee they made when they had returned earlier. Two of them were sitting in chairs, and two were on the sofa. They listened to the fire pop and crack as the wood slowly burned to warm them from the dampness that had overtaken the port. Sasha sat in her chair on the far side of the fireplace and faced a window on the opposite side of the cabin. Through the window, she had a clear view of the second cabin. All four carried on a conversation about all they found at the homestead. Some even mentioned that it appeared like a storm was moving into the area.

Throughout the entire conversation, Sasha kept an eye on the occupants across the way. She realized that, so far, the only two crew members she had witnessed in the cabin were Tim and Elaine.

"What are you staring at, Sasha?" Dave asked.

Sasha never quit staring out the window. After a second or two, Sasha answered, "As we've been sitting here talking, I've been watching the other cabin. I've only seen two people the entire time — Tim and Elaine. So far, Mark and Andre haven't been visible at all. I don't think they are still at the cabin."

"Where would they have gone?" Betty asked.

Sasha turned to Betty with a puzzled facial expression. "I don't know. But why ain't the other group back yet? Shouldn't they have started back when the mist began to fall?"

Willy stood and looked out the window behind Sasha that faced toward the meadow. "I haven't said anything, but I was wondering about the other group myself."

"Okay, people, let's not overreact about this, I mean—" Dave raised his hands and extended his fingers.

He was interrupted by Betty.

"Wait a minute, Dave. I don't think we are overreacting. It's starting to get darker outside, especially with the rain clouds moving in. Pretty soon, it's going to be difficult to even see out there, and I agree, why aren't the others back yet?"

Willy walked over to the window and looked out.

"Betty's right," Willy said. "The light is fading pretty fast, and it's going to start raining any minute. Maybe we should go over to the other cabin and see if they have at least heard from the others."

Dave stood up from his seat and held out his hands toward the fire to help his chill. "Tell you what, people. The three of you go next door and see what you can find out. I'll stay and guard the ole warm fire."

Sasha, Betty, and Willy put on their rain jackets, each grabbing a flashlight, and headed for the door. Willy turned toward Dave as they exited the cabin to say, "Last chance not to be left alone, ole boy."

"Thanks, but I'll just hang out here till you get back," Dave said with a smile. "Happy trails, buddy, and for goodness sakes, don't let the boogeyman get you."

Willy shut the door, and the three of them carefully navigated down the wet steps. They noticed the mist was getting heavier and a breeze had started to blow. They slowly walked the slippery path between the cabins and made their way up the steps to the door. Sasha turned the knob and found it to be locked.

*That's odd*, she thought, *since we haven't locked the contestants' door once before dark from the time we arrived here.* Sasha knocked on the door.

Elaine jumped out of her chair and rushed to the door. She twisted the deadbolt and unlocked the doorknob. Everyone on the deck heard both clicks, and Elaine opened the door. There stood the three contestants. Elaine moved to the side, and they entered the cabin.

Everyone took notice that Elaine immediately secured both locks once the door was shut. Willy noticed Tim removing his hand from his pistol as they entered the room.

They all removed their jackets.

"Have you heard from the others?" Betty asked quickly. "We were getting a little worried since they haven't returned yet."

Willy noticed Elaine glanced at Tim.

"What's the deal, people?" Willy asked. "Why did you look over at Tim, Elaine? What's going on here?"

Neither Tim nor Elaine spoke. Elaine just stared at Tim.

Tim and Willy eyes met with a stare. Elaine and Tim knew the contestants had a right to know what was going on, but what about the show?

"Okay," Willy said. "I get the feeling that you people know something we don't. First off, both locks on the door were secured, and it's not completely dark yet. Plus, when we came through the door, you had a hand on that pistol, Tim. Let's hear it now, guys."

Tim looked at Elaine. He stood at the radio and picked up the walkie-talkie. He tried, again, to radio Bill. Everyone stood in silence waiting for the response...but it never came.

Tim switched channels on the radio and keyed the device. "Mark, this is Tim. You got me, buddy?"

\*\*\*

Mark and Andre had moved down the mountain a small distance after covering Mr. Long's body when the radio came to life again. It startled both of them. Mark unclipped the radio and answered, "Loud and clear, Tim. What's up?"

"I've tried several times to contact Bill and the other team, but I can't get an answer, Mark," Tim responded. "It's not like Bill to turn off the radio. And the SAT Phone isn't acquiring satellites. I guess the storm is messing with it."

"Well, give us a little bit, and we'll be back," Mark said. "We can assess what action to take then."

"Willy, Sasha, and Betty are here, Mark. They know something is not right," Tim informed him.

Mark looked over at Andre and raised his eyebrows. "Tell them what we know. I don't think we need to be concerned about the show anymore. We've already lost one person. Everybody stays together till we get back, and when the other group gets back, all of you stay in one cabin."

"Roger that," Tim replied. Tim laid the walkie-talkie back on the table.

Sasha stepped up to the table and asked, "What did Mark mean when he said we had already lost one person?"

Tim looked around at the others. Tim explained how there was another player in the game — Mr. Long. He explained that Mr. Long's job was to provide a certain fear factor to the contestants for the show. He explained that the only contact that they had with him was the SAT Phone and a locator. He continued to share with the group that the monitor was showing Mr. Long's transmitter in a fixed position on the mountainside. He informed the group that they tried to reach him on the phone but never got an answer, and that Mark and Andre took the locator monitor to locate the transmitter.

"When Mark and Andre found the transmitter, they also found Mr. Long," Tim said. "His injuries were similar to what you guys found at the homestead."

"His body was torn apart?" Betty gasped in astonishment.

"I don't know for sure," Tim answered. "He only said his injuries were similar. That's all I know, people."

Sasha sat down and stared into the fireplace. Fear ripped through her.

"Oh my gosh, what about the others?" Sasha asked.

"I've got a gun," Tim assured her. "Mark and Bill have a gun, also. When Mark, Andre, and the others get back, we'll ride out the storm together. When the weather breaks, we'll call Rob, and they can bring the boat. We'll leave as a group and get out of this place."

Willy and Betty joined Sasha and sat down at the fireplace. The three of them sat silently, trying to process everything they had just learned.

\*\*\*

Moving down the shoreline was a slow process for Shelly and Ronnie. With each step, they were painstakingly careful of their footing. Even though the ground below their feet was relatively sturdy, there were plenty of obstacles to overcome. The amount of driftwood lying on the shore had increased dramatically. There were plenty of rocks for one to slip on and twist an ankle. So, they focused on their footing as they progressed down the shore. Occasionally, one of them would hear a noise from above in the woods that reminded them that they were not alone.

Shelley felt the dampness slowly penetrate her clothing, and it sent a chill through her body. She didn't complain. She knew that, as uncomfortable as she was, it was nothing compared to what Ronnie was enduring. Both wanted to get safely back to the warmth of the cabins. They realized that they would be spending at least part of the night in the darkness, traversing the shoreline, and had to be very careful.

Shelley halted, turned, faced Ronnie, and said, "We're not going to make it back for quite some time, Ronnie. I'm not even sure how far we got to go. Let's take a break and rest for a minute. I know this is difficult for you, and I'm tired myself, and I'm not carrying extra weight like you."

Ronnie took a couple of steps and slowly lowered Stan onto the wet bark of a fallen tree. He leaned against the tree and confirmed, "It's gonna be tough to get down the shore once it gets dark, Shelley."

"Yeah, I know. We'll just take our time, Ronnie, but we'll get there."

"Yes, we will," Ronnie agreed and nodded.

Neither one of them looked up into the woods, not even for a single glance. Shelley vividly remembered what Ronnie had said about making eye contact.

"Ronnie, whatever is following us is merely keeping pace and staying out of sight," Shelley said. "Why?"

"I'm not sure, Shelley. It doesn't make sense. Whatever it is, I think it's just watching us. It's the *why* part that I can't seem to figure out." Ronnie peered across the water.

"When you were a kid, and something chased you boys down the mountain that day, did it try to catch you?" Shelley asked.

"No," Ronnie said. "It got pretty close, but it never fully approached us. It seemed to maintain the same distance between us and itself, almost like the thing merely wanted us out of the area."

Shelley glanced at Stan and then back over to Ronnie and said, "I don't get it, Ronnie. If it's the same thing that was at the meadow, why did it kill Stan?"

"I don't know, Shelley," Ronnie said. "I just don't know. Let's go a little farther before it gets totally dark." He pushed himself off the tree, turned, and hoisted Stan back on his shoulder.

Shelley came to her feet from resting on the rock, stuck her hands in her coat pockets to adjust it, and found the flashlight she had placed in there earlier. She removed the light and showed it to Ronnie and said, "I forgot I had put this in my coat."

"That's great, Shelley. Glad you thought to bring one," Ronnie said.

"Old habit of mine. I carry a small one everywhere I go." Shelley patted Ronnie's arm. "I don't like to be caught in the dark. Let's go."

As soon as the pair started their journey again down the shore, they heard the small twig snap in the woods above them. Neither one of them looked up into the forest. It didn't really surprise either one of them. Both fully expected that whatever was shadowing them would continue with them on their journey. It would be the one to decide what the night's outcome would be.

***

Back at the crew's cabin, the minutes kept ticking by slowly. Tim sat at the table and stared at the phone and the radio. There were no signal bars on the phone. It was not picking up any satellites. He hoped that any minute Bill's voice would come through the radio to verify they were okay, but the only sounds he heard were the crackling of the fire and the sound of Elaine's footsteps as she walked to the kitchen.

Elaine got a bottle of water and twisted the cap. She took a sip of water and walked back toward the fireplace. The sound of an object striking the roof startled everyone.

Betty jumped to her feet and wheeled around to face the others. Elaine stopped almost in mid-stride.

"What was that?" Betty whispered.

"I don't know," Tim said cautiously. "Maybe the wind blew out a limb, and it hit the roof." He placed his hand on the pistol and gripped it tightly.

"Number one, there aren't any trees close enough to the cabin for a limb to fall out of and hit the roof," Willy said quietly. "Number two, that sounded more like a rock or something."

There was a second thump on the roof. This time, it was unmistakable that the sound came from above the bedroom area. The sound of the object was tumbling down the shingles. It impacted the deck with a thud. The cabin fell silent. Everyone tried to process what had just happened. Then, they heard another sound — the pitter patter of the rain as it started to fall and hit the roof. No one spoke. Everyone stood still and listened.

Sasha, frozen where she stood, looked from one window to the other. She caught sight of Dave as he moved from the sitting area to the kitchen.

"Hey, guys, what about Dave?" Sasha asked.

"We probably shouldn't leave him over there alone. I'll go and get him," Willy said.

"You heard Mark; let's all stay together," Tim said. "We need to get his attention and have him lock the door or make a mad dash over here."

"We have the gun, Tim. We need to do something," Elaine said.

"We'll signal him with the flashlight and get his attention," Sasha said carefully. "We can motion for him to come over here, and once he starts walking to the cabin, we can open our door and guard him until he gets here."

Willy went to the window and aimed the flashlight at the contestants' cabin window. He signaled Dave with the flashlight.

Dave exited the kitchen and caught sight of the flashing light coming from across the way. He slowly made his way to the window. He took a sip of his freshly poured coffee. He raised his free hand in a gesture to indicate he was enjoying his cup of coffee.

Sasha joined Willy at the window, and both waved their hands to tell Dave to come over. Dave pointed to the cup and indicated he'd be there as soon as he finished the coffee. Willy and Sasha frantically repeated the gestures with more urgency. Dave didn't see them. He had turned from the window and walked to his seat by the fire.

Dave murmured out loud, "Those crazy people think I'm gonna waste a good cup of coffee and come out in the rain. They've lost their minds."

Dave ambled back to the fireplace and placed another log on the fire. He sat down in the chair with his coffee. Before taking the next sip, he inhaled the bold aroma of the fresh brew. He took a satisfying sip and relaxed back into the chair.

Sasha and Willy stood at the window. Sasha stomped her foot against the wooden floor in frustration.

"What was that all about?" Sasha asked with irritation.

"Why does he have to be so hardheaded?" Willy asked with impatience. "When we came over here, he didn't want to come, and he said that he was going to guard the fire."

"Well, then he made his choice," Betty snarled.

"I don't think we should just leave him over there alone," Elaine interjected.

Betty walked over to Tim and placed both of her hands on the table.

"Listen, I don't like the fact that Dave is over there alone either, but he had the option of coming with us, and I kind of got the impression that he thought we were being silly coming over here in the first place," Betty said firmly. "Willy even tried a second time, going out the door, and Dave flatly refused."

"I agree," Sasha said and moved to the table. She was interrupted by Elaine.

"Wait a minute, Sasha," Elaine said harshly. "You were the one that brought Dave up in the first place, and then stomped your foot when he turned away from the window."

"I realize that, Elaine, but if he's not willing to make an effort, should someone take a chance going outside?" Sasha asked defensively and stood up.

"Alright, everybody, let's remain calm," Tim instructed. "The next time Dave gets up, we'll try to signal him again. Willy, if you don't care, watch for Dave to move around, and let us know when he gets up. If we can get his attention, all of us will signal this time for him to come over. Maybe he'll take heed if we motion as a group."

Willy glanced out the window.

"Right now, all I can see is his hand holding the cup on the end table beside the chair," Willy said and looked toward Tim.

"Just signal him when he gets up," Tim instructed.

# CHAPTER 14

Mark and Andre reached the point of the mountain where it started to decline at a much steeper rate. Both men briefly remembered how happy they were when they arrived at this section climbing up. The mist had given way to a steady rain, and the raindrops pounding the forest floor were deafening.

They heard the wind whipping across the high mountain tops around them. In the distance, there was the occasional flash of lightning. The visibility in the woods was quickly becoming less and less. Their coats provided protection from the elements, but they knew if the conditions got worse, neither one of them had a lot of confidence in their attire.

"It's gonna be pretty slick going off this mountain, Andre," Mark said. "Be careful where you step." He stopped and leaned his shoulder against a small tree.

"Yeah, I just want to get off this mountain and get back to the cabin," Andre said. "Let's get moving."

Slowly they started down the mountainside. They carefully placed each step in the proper place. It was a tedious trek keeping upright and maneuvering around the obstacles that laid in their way.

They heard a single *whoop* from above them, high on the mountain. Another one came from the mountain to their left. Mark and Andre both skidded a couple of feet on the wet leaves and finally came to a stop. Mark turned and looked behind them up the mountain. Andre scanned to the left.

Another loud howl came from above them. It was so loud that it felt like it vibrated the men's bodies as the sound echoed around them.

Mark turned and faced back down the mountain.

"Andre, they know we are here," Mark said in a panic. "We've got to get off this mountain as fast as we can! Don't stop for any reason!"

Both men erupted in their effort to escape. They were on their feet and sometimes on their rear ends, sliding down the mountain. Neither one was paying much attention to the placement of their steps now. They were on and off their feet. The men crashed down the mountainside at a frantic rate. They grabbed at small saplings here and there to regain a small amount of control.

They heard two loud grunts directly in front of them. Andre was the first to see the creature. He had never seen anything that large standing on two feet. Even though the lighting in the forest had grown dim, Andre could see the massive structure of this thing, and it was covered in hair. There was no time to think.

Andre firmly planted his left foot into the soil. He lunged to his right as the creature extended his left arm to grab him. The creature missed Andre. The hairy creature swiftly rotated his body, swinging its right arm. The blow struck Mark at his right shoulder, sending him careening off the mountain's end.

Mark had lost control of his descent. He tumbled completely out of control toward the old, abandoned road. His head struck the side of a log. He lost consciousness and drifted slowly into darkness.

*\*\**

Dave was totally mesmerized as he stared into the fire. The small flames danced in and around the logs as the wood slowly burned. Dave drifted into daydreaming about how, when he got back to Ohio, he'd try to pitch the idea to his wife of selling their house and building a cabin like this.

Even though his wife wasn't much of an outdoor person, he might be able to convince her of the idea, especially if they built it just outside of their small hometown. They could be away from almost everyone, yet still be close enough for her to drive into town and meet her girlfriends for their shopping excursions. He wasn't sure if he could pull it off, but it was definitely worth a try.

Dave's daydreaming was interrupted by a *creak* sound from outside. It sounded like someone was coming up the steps and moving towards the door of the cabin. He waited patiently for the door to open. He assumed the three from next door had returned. The door never swung open. *Now what?* Dave thought.

He clearly heard someone walking from the steps to the door. *Where did they go? What were they doing standing on the deck in the rain?*

Dave rose from the chair and approached the door. He turned the knob and opened the door. Nobody was there. *Were the other three playing a joke on him?* Dave thought. He leaned his head out the door and surveyed the deck. He was sure that he heard something, but there was nobody there.

Dave grabbed his jacket hanging on the wooden peg beside the door, quickly put it on, and stepped outside. Dave tried to look out over the bay, but the light was fading fast. He couldn't see the other side. Dave could barely see the edge of the water on their side of the bay below the cabins. He noticed the pungent odor that filled the air around him. It was as unpleasant as the smell of a skunk trying to defend itself from a predator.

This odor was much different. It was much worse than the smell of a skunk or a wet dog. This odor filled the entire area around the cabins. Dave slowly moved to the side of the cabin, which faced toward the meadow. He wondered, *Why hasn't the second group returned? Surely, they should be back by now.*

Dave decided to walk over to the other cabin and check on things. He turned to go back and shut the door before heading over to the others. A loud thud on the deck startled Dave. He wheeled around toward the noise. He placed one hand firmly on the deck railing. He didn't expect to see what was standing there. Dave froze in his stance.

With two giant steps, the hairy figure grabbed Dave by the throat. This creature lifted Dave two or three feet off the deck floor. The pressure on Dave's throat was immense. He tried desperately to pry the creature's fingers away, but the creature's powerful grip was unmovable. Dave knew his throat would give way and collapse. The creature hurled him from the deck, and his body crashed through the saplings and brush below the cabin. The impact almost knocked Dave unconscious. Everything seemed to be in slow motion. Dave heard something closing in on him from both sides. He realized that there were two of these things.

The first creature picked Dave up by gripping his head with one hand. Dave felt the creature's warm air on the back of his neck, and a grunt emerged from its mouth. The big hairy figure slammed Dave's head into the saplings. It released its grip and let Dave fall to the ground. The second creature raised one of its legs and stomped Dave's head with crushing force. Dave's body went totally limp, lying in the wet brush below the cabin. The first hairy figure that had approached Dave from beside the cabin wrapped its mighty fingers around Dave's wrist and partially lifted his body.

The second figure leaned down and smelled Dave's dead body. It gripped Dave's other arm and let loose a growl that split the night's air. The two creatures tugged and pulled on Dave's body until his left arm finally gave way at the elbow. The severed portion of the arm was then thrown into the air. It propelled to the top of the deck railing and ricocheted to the outside of the cabin wall. It came to rest against the cabin on the deck floor.

The second creature continued to violently swing Dave's body around by Dave's other arm with a firm grip. Dave's body was slammed against anything that was in close proximity. This continued for a few seconds until Dave's shoulder ripped from its socket, and his body was thrown down the hillside below the cabin. The large, hairy figure tossed the arm toward Dave's body. The creature arched its back and raised its arms high in the air above its head, and with a bellowing howl, it roared through the trees and the hills around the cabins.

"What was that?" Betty shouted and jumped to her feet.

"Some kind of animal, a big animal," Willy said with fear in his voice and fright in his eyes. "Maybe the exact animal we came here to find proof of. I don't think this is a game anymore."

"Whoa, Willy, let's not get all worked up here," Tim said. "It could have been a bear or something. We don't know what that was." He raised up his hands in submission, but he continued to stare out at the window at the other cabin.

Everyone became silent. They waited to hear any other howls. There were no more sounds of any kind except for the steady downpour of the rain hitting the roof of the cabin.

"Willy, do you see Dave?" Tim asked slowly.

"The coffee cup is still on the end table, but I haven't seen Dave for a while," Willy answered. "Not for a few minutes."

"Then where is he?" Sasha asked.

"I don't know," Willy replied with uncertainty. "He could have dozed off in the chair. If he got up, I guess I could've missed him."

"Missed him?" Betty asked. "How could you have missed him? You were watching him through the window."

"Betty, all I could see was his arm and the coffee cup," Willy said defensively. "If he got out of the chair and moved to the right, I would never know."

"Surely, if he's awake, he heard the exact same thing we did," Tim said. "He must be asleep or else he would've got up and moved around in the cabin."

"Anybody ever hear something like that before?" Elaine asked. "Betty, you're from Michigan. Lots of woods there, right?"

"Yeah, lots of woods in Michigan," Betty answered.

"Well, have you ever heard anything like that or know someone who has?" Elaine asked and hoped for reassurance.

"I haven't heard anything like that, but I've heard tales of things that possibly walk in the woods," Betty said. "You know, you hear people say things. I know this guy who was out hunting, and he heard strange noises and saw something moving through the forest, and they can't explain it. But personally, no, I've never heard anything like that."

"How about the rest of you?" Elaine asked. "Has anybody ever heard a noise like that?"

"Listen, people, the last thing we need to do is frighten ourselves," Tim said. "We should be safe in this cabin from anything that might be out there." He tried to reassure himself as well as the others.

"I don't think we're doing anything but being realistic," Sasha said. "Mark and Andre discovered Mr. Long's body out in the woods, and most of us didn't even know he existed until the radio call. I assume he was quite comfortable with the outdoors, and he was out here alone, right?"

"Yes, he was an avid outdoorsman," Tim said. "Some type of a survivalist, I suppose."

"Well, obviously he didn't have a problem walking around out here in the wilderness by himself, but something happened to him," Sasha said. "The other team is not back yet, and it's now dark outside. Tim, the second team is not answering the radio. Something is not right."

Tim picked up the walkie-talkie and keyed the channel for Bill and the second team. He said, "Bill, this is Tim, do you copy?"

There was no response.

"Bill, this is Tim, come in Bill," Tim said again.

Everyone waited in silence, but there was no reply. Tim switched the channel to call Mark, keyed the radio, and said, "Mark, can you hear me buddy?"

Mark did not reply back. He laid unconscious in the wet leaves. Tim tried again to reach Mark.

"Mark, come in, Mark...Can you hear me, Mark?"

The signal transmitted perfectly through the radio and broke the silence of the darkness on the side of the mountain. Mark was in no condition to hear or answer it.

Tim sat at the table, holding the radio in one hand and supporting his head with the other. His elbow rested on the shiny wood of the dining table.

"Sasha is right, something is wrong," Willy said. "These people didn't just leave this place long ago because of some hocus pocus they dreamed up in their heads. There is something here, and it is very much alive. It walks through these woods. This is its home. Don't you see? We have infringed on its territory. This thing or things are just protecting what's theirs...just like when the fishing village was here."

"Okay, let's say this Hairy Man is for real. What do we do?" Betty asked apprehensively.

"We stay in this cabin just like Mark said and stay together and watch out for each other," Tim instructed.

"But what if some of the others need help?" Elaine asked.

"Elaine, I'm worried about the others also," Sasha said. "I don't understand why they are out there, and we are here, but I think Tim is right. We can't reach anyone on the radio, and the SAT Phone will not pick up satellites. We don't know exactly where anyone outside of this cabin is. The only people we can account for is us and Dave next door. If we went looking for the others, it would be like hunting for a needle in a haystack."

"I agree. We wouldn't even know where to begin to search for anyone," Willy added.

"I just know if I was out there, I'd like for somebody to come for me," Elaine said.

"Even if you were no longer alive," Tim said and looked up from the table. It was the first time he agreed with the same conclusions as the rest of the group.

Everyone paused for a second and stared at Tim.

"We can't risk it unless someone calls us on that radio," Betty said. "I say we stay put."

"Elaine, if one person calls on that walkie-talkie, I promise I will go look, okay?" Willy said.

"Okay, Willy, I know you guys are right," Elaine agreed. "It's just a very difficult situation."

Willy turned and focused on the window of the other cabin. He still did not see a sign of Dave, and all he could see was the coffee cup sitting on the end table by the chair.

# CHAPTER 15

Shelley and Ronnie continued to make their way down the shoreline toward the cabins. The progress slowed dramatically. It had become more difficult. The darkness had overtaken the port, and the steady downpour of the rain had tremendously dampened their spirits. Both were becoming more and more exhausted as they fought to put one foot in front of the other.

Shelley tried to walk beside Ronnie, shining her flashlight on the ground in front of them. Walking side by side became increasingly difficult. The tide began to come in, and the amount of shoreline to walk on was shrinking every few minutes. Less and less of the soil that they desperately needed to step on remained as they inched along their journey.

"Shelley, I've got to rest for a minute," Ronnie said and broke the silence of the night.

Both of them found large rocks to sit on. Shelley sat on hers first, but she didn't turn off the flashlight. Ronnie placed Stan's body on another rock. He sat down beside him to rest. The movement that was near them in the forest ceased the very minute they sat down. Ronnie took a couple of deep breaths.

"Shelley, you can turn off the flashlight," Ronnie said. "We're gonna need it to get back, so let's save the batteries."

Shelley clicked the button on the light, then pushed the hood of her jacket off her head. She adjusted the hair from covering her eyes.

"Why does it keep following us, Ronnie?" Shelley asked. "Why doesn't it just do whatever it's going to do and get it over with?"

"I don't have an answer to that question either, Shelley. All I know is that we're going down this shoreline, and it's shadowing us as we move. Let's just keep doing exactly what we've been doing so far and see what happens."

Shelley repositioned the hood to shield her head and neck from the rain.

"The tide is coming in pretty quick, Ronnie," she said. "We can barely navigate the shore now. If the water gets a little higher, it's going to be tough to walk at all, and we won't be able to see where we're stepping."

"Yeah, I know, Shelley," Ronnie said. "But I've noticed a couple of game trails coming down to the shore from the mountainside. I guess it's where animals come down looking for an easy meal when it's low tide."

"Wait a minute, Ronnie. You surely are not suggesting we venture up into the woods with whatever is following us?" Shelley asked with surprise.

"We're not gonna be able to walk down here if it's covered with water," Ronnie explained. "I'll never carry Stan and be able to blindly step as we move. Whatever is in those woods could have jumped us at any time, but for some reason, it hasn't. I don't know why, but I think it'll continue to follow us on a game trail. Maybe a game trail will lead us back up to the old road. That sure would be easier walking."

"I don't know about going into the woods, Ronnie," Shelley said. "What if that thing views that as an act of aggression?"

"I don't think it will, Shelley. We have to find a trail if we are going to continue."

"Maybe you're right, but I don't like the idea of being in the woods with it," Shelley said reluctantly.

"Keep doing the same thing we've been doing down the shore," Ronnie said. "If you hear something, don't shine the flashlight in the direction of it. Don't even look in the direction of the noise. Just keep looking forward or at the ground no matter what happens."

"Well, let's go a little farther and find that trail," Shelley said and clicked on the flashlight again. She stood.

Ronnie came to his feet and stretched his back. He grabbed Stan's arm and slowly rotated him up on his shoulders. The pair slowly made their way once again. Shelley assumed the position on Ronnie's left side and shone the flashlight in front of them. After several minutes of struggling along the shore and as the water closed in and eliminated what little ground was left to walk on, Ronnie spotted bear tracks in the wet soil. The tracks no longer moved along the shore but headed up the bank into the trees. Ronnie stopped and motioned for Shelley to follow the tracks with the light. She guided the light and followed the tracks up to the tree line. There was a game trail that led into the forest.

"I guess this is our trail?" Shelley whispered. "It could intersect to the old road somewhere."

"I think so, Shelley," Ronnie said. "Even though our friend is still with us, nothing has happened yet. We've really got no choice. We can't continue on the shoreline."

"Can you make it with Stan?" Shelley asked.

"I'll manage somehow. We're not gonna leave him now," Ronnie replied.

Shelley left the last of the shore as she grabbed a low hanging limb and pulled herself onto the trail. She turned, stuck the flashlight in her mouth, and reached out her hand to Ronnie. He firmly grasped Shelley's hand while he supported Stan with the other. Together they managed to conquer the small incline, and both stood firmly on the trail.

As far they could tell, the path angled up the side of the mountain at a gradual rate. Shelley didn't dare shine the light much ahead of their position. They started slowly up the trail. Both realized that the thing was still shadowing them and intended to continue along with them. Shelley took a couple of steps and shone the light for Ronnie to take a couple of steps. It was a slow process, but at least there were not as many obstacles as there were down on the shore.

\*\*\*

The confusion in Mark's mind ran rampant as he began to regain consciousness. *Where am I? Why is my face wet? Why is it so dark? What happened?* Mark laid there with no movement. He slowly began to recall the events of Andre and him going down the mountain. He remembered the sounds of the grunts and the howls on the mountain above them. He recalled the creature that they met coming down the steep section of the mountain. He remembered how something struck him. He recalled how he lost control and recklessly tumbled down the mountain. *How long have I been unconscious? Where is Andre?*

Mark tried to reposition himself and lean against the tree that had stopped his careening through the forest. A sharp pain shot through his lower left leg. Luckily, his backpack was on his back. He painstaking maneuvered the straps off his back while fighting the pain in his leg. Mark opened the pack and fumbled around in search of his flashlight. After a few seconds, he located it. He clicked the switch on the light and aimed it toward his foot.

His foot was not pointed in the correct direction. Mark leaned back and dropped his arm down by his side. He caught a glimpse of Andre's boots. He slowly shone the light toward Andre's boots. He shone the light up Andre's body up to his head. Andre's eyes were wide open, blankly staring into the night. Andre's head and neck were laid in an unnatural state in conjunction to the rest of his body. Mark realized that Andre's neck was broken. Andre had not been as fortunate as Mark. Mark was in bad shape, but he was alive.

Mark clutched the pack with one hand and used the other to pull himself through the wet leaves over to Andre's body. Mark removed a survival blanket from the pack and covered Andre as best he could. He placed his hand on Andre's hand, sat there, and held it tightly.

Mark concluded that none of them were going to leave this place alive. Mark sat there and thought, *These creatures that everybody thought were dreamed up were very much real. Andre and I heard their vocalizations, and now, we encountered one of them on this mountain. We were not dreaming. Mr. Long is dead, and now Andre is dead.*

Mark was giving up hope of making it back to the cabin. He knew that they should have called Rob about the transmitter and not being able to reach Mr. Long on the SAT Phone, but it was now too late to second guess what they had done. Mark grabbed the backpack and pulled it on his lap. He fumbled with the light until he found the walkie-talkie radio. He thought, *I hope this thing still works.* Mark keyed the radio and said in a weak voice, "Tim, this is Mark, do you read me?"

Back at the cabin, Willy monitored the cabin next door. Tim was sitting at the table and stared at the pistol. Sasha and Betty were seated at end of the fireplace. Elaine slowly paced back and forth. When Mark's voice came through the radio, everyone was startled and turned to the table.

Tim grabbed the radio. "Got you loud and clear, Mark. Where are you guys?"

"Listen to me, Tim," Mark said in a low voice. "These creatures are real. We've seen one of them. Did the other group get back yet?"

"No, not yet," Tim said, pushing the button.

"If they aren't back by now, I don't think they will be coming back," Mark said sadly. "Has anything happened there?"

Tim glanced at the others. Everyone heard what Mark had just said.

"We've had some kind of objects, maybe rocks, hit the roof of the cabin," Tim said. "A little while later, there was some type of howl we heard outside. Not sure what it was. It was like something none of us have ever heard."

"We heard a loud, bellowing howl directly above us, right after we heard some grunting sounds in the woods," Mark said urgently. "We tried to get off this mountain, and we ran straight into one of them. Tim, these things are massive...maybe eight or nine feet tall. All of you should stay in the cabin. Call Rob the minute the SAT Phone picks up satellite signals."

"Where's Andre?" Tim asked cautiously.

Mark paused for a second and hesitated before he answered.

"When we came off the mountain, I think the creature knocked me off my feet. I don't know if the creature did the same thing to Andre or not. I must have been unconscious for a while. But anyway, when I came to, Andre was lying next to me in the leaves." Mark choked on his words. He regained his composure and continued, "Tim, it looks like Andre broke his neck during the fall."

Everyone in the cabin bowed down their heads in disbelief except Elaine.

"Can Mark make it back?" Elaine asked.

Tim keyed the radio again and asked, "You gonna start making your way back? Do we need to come and meet you?"

Mark stared into the darkness. He knew that no one could help him.

"No, Tim, I believe my ankle is broken. I'm just gonna sit here with Andre."

"Mark, we aren't just going to leave you out there," Tim said.

"Listen to me, Tim," Mark said. "I'm not totally sure if I am alone out here right now. It's best if you guys remain in the safety of the cabin. Once daylight comes, I'll call you back on the radio, and you can come get me, okay?"

"It's gonna be a little while before daylight, Mark," Tim said.

"I'll be alright, Tim. Just wait for me to call. Over and out." Mark ended the conversation.

"Over and out, Mark," Tim said slowly.

Mark knew he was not alone in the damp forest. The musky odor he smelled assured him of that. He slid closer to Andre's body and wrapped his arms around him. Mark pulled Andre onto his lap the best his strength would allow.

"Andre, you came out here with me, my friend," Mark said. "I will not leave you now." He held tightly onto Andre's body.

Mark turned off the flashlight and leaned back against a small sapling that bent back just enough, as if he was relaxing in a recliner. Not quite as comfortable, but not too bad for being out in the middle of the forest. Mark sat there holding Andre and listened to the raindrops hitting the ground. The odor still filled the moist air, and every now and then, Mark was sure he could hear the creature breathe.

The sound was like when a person would breathe in deeply and slowly exhale air. The breathing sound reminded Mark of how a doctor would press their cold stethoscope against your chest or back and ask you to breathe in and out.

*Why was it just standing or sitting there? What was it waiting on? Why didn't it just get this over with?* Mark hadn't checked for his pistol, but it was probably no match for whatever was watching him. He wasn't sure if there was just one, or more. Mark didn't know, but he knew he wasn't going to shine the light to find out. Mark checked the pack again to see if there was anything else he could use for protection from the elements. He was surprised when he found another survival blanket. He removed the small box that contained the blanket. He tore open the plastic wrap and spread the blanket over him and Andre's head, much like a small tarp, to protect them. He decided he would wait for whatever unfolded in the darkness of the forest.

\*\*\*

Back at the command center, the captain and Rob monitored the storm.

"Looks like we are gonna get lucky with this storm, buddy," the captain said and patted Rob on the shoulder.

"Yep, she's starting to break up a little and may even clear out completely by mid-morning at the port," Rob said with a smile. "Still gonna be a little rain and probably some wind through the night, but tomorrow will be a much brighter day."

The captain raised his cup. Nobody was quite sure of what extra boost the captain added to his coffee, but all of them were pretty sure it had a little more punch to it than just the caffeine.

"I'm not gonna lie to you boys, I was a little concerned about her earlier," the captain said and took a long sip. He squinted his eyes, not from the temperature of the coffee, but from the punch of the extra boost he added.

The editing producer stopped pacing around the room and sat down in a large swivel chair.

"I feel a lot better now," the producer said. "This could have turned out bad for everyone if this storm had gotten worse instead of better." He rested his arms on the chair.

Rob stood and faced the producer.

"You're a pretty big worry wart, man, but I know what you mean," Rob said. "It would have been difficult to reach them in an emergency."

"Not difficult, Rob," the captain said. "Impossible. The only way in or out is by boat. You might fly in a float plane, I suspect. But in a storm, you're just not getting to those people."

"Well, thankfully the storm isn't going to be severe enough to bother anyone," Rob said. "But I do think that as soon as the cloud cover breaks up and we can get satellite signals on the phone, I'll call and check on everyone."

"I would appreciate that, Rob, and that would make me feel a lot better," the editing producer said before continuing with a smirk, "being the worry wart I am, you know."

All three men smiled. Rob turned and faced the weather monitor to make sure he and the captain were right. He thought, *All seems to be looking up for those at the port.*

The captain poured himself a fresh cup of coffee and slipped his hand into his jacket's pocket, removed the flask containing his special ingredient. He poured it in to his liking, returned the flask to his jacket, and sat down in a large, soft chair. He looked up and saw the producer and Rob staring at him.

The captain raised the cup as if to make a toast, and all three men chuckled. Everyone in the room leaned back in their seats and breathed a sigh of relief. They took turns watching the storm on the monitor. They planned to call the port first thing in the morning, when the storm passed.

# CHAPTER 16

Willy took one more look out the window and stared next door. There was still nothing to see but the cup resting on the end table. Willy closed his eyes and clinched them shut. He took a deep breath and slowly exhaled the air. He opened his eyes, turned, and walked into the kitchen area. He opened the drawers of the cabinets and rummaged through them.

In the cooking utensil drawer, Willy removed the largest knife he saw in the silverware plastic container. He continued his search through the remaining drawers. He opened drawers, moved objects, and closed drawers. He repeated this process as he made his way throughout the entire kitchen.

Everyone remained seated as they were before Mark's voice emerged from the radio, except for Elaine. Elaine was not seated and was the only one who was intently watching Willy. The others glimpsed at his actions but simply dropped their heads to return to their own thoughts.

"Willy, what are you doing?" Elaine asked, interrupting the others' thoughts.

"I'm looking for some things I'm gonna need," Willy said. "Has anyone seen a tarp or maybe one of those old vinyl tablecloths? You know, the kind our parents used at picnics or maybe even on the dining room table?"

"What do you need one of them for?" Tim asked and looked at Willy.

"I'm going to get Mark and Andre," Willy answered calmly.

"What?" Betty interjected. "Willy, you can't go out there. Mark said to wait till morning, and he would call." She rose from sitting at the end of the fireplace hearth.

"I'll go with you, Willy," Elaine quickly said.

"No, Elaine. You guys are going to stay put in this cabin," Tim ordered. "I have a gun to protect all of you."

"If I can make it to Mark, he has a weapon, too, right?" Willy asked.

"Yes, he has a pistol, but I'm not sure about you going out there," Tim said. "I think you should wait till morning when Mark calls back."

"What are you going to do?" Willy asked rudely. "Shoot me as I go through the door? I told Elaine that if anyone's voice came through that radio, I would go to help them. I meant it then and I mean it now."

"I think someone should go with you, Willy," Sasha said.

"Sasha, I don't want you guys traipsing down the old road in the dark, out there with who knows what," Willy said. "I think I can find Mark since he has a flashlight too."

"There's a tarp in one of the equipment bags to protect all the stuff in case we needed to," Tim informed Willy. "I don't understand what good it's going to do you, though."

"I'll need the tarp to place Andre on to slide him on the road," Tim said. "Mark and I can make it down the old road since it's relatively flat, and with the rain on the leaves and dirt, it should slide fairly easy."

"What about getting Mark up the road if his ankle is broken?" Elaine said. "He's not gonna be able to just walk, you know."

"We'll need to stabilize his leg and make a splint for it somehow," Willy said.

"There's some rope in the equipment bag," Tim interjected.

"Take the end table legs, and you can take the rope and tie the wooden supports on each side of his ankle," Elaine suggested. "That should temporarily hold it in place, but he still can't walk on it."

"He can put one arm around my neck and hop," Willy said. "If I have to, I'll drag them both back. Tim, get the rope and tarp for me, and bring me that end table, Betty."

Willy broke off the end table legs and laid them next to his backpack. Elaine left the room with Tim and returned shortly with the medical supplies. She unzipped the carrying case and began to set some small bottles on the table.

"Mark will need something for pain, plus I have some low-level antibiotics to give him as a precautionary," Elaine insisted.

Elaine removed three small clear containers. She placed the antibiotics in one container and made two doses of pain medicine in the small bottles. She wrapped a piece of gauze tape around the bottle with the antibiotics so Willy could tell the difference between the pain medicine and the antibiotics. She retrieved three bottles of water from the kitchen and placed the pill bottles in a plastic bag. She zipped it shut and placed all she had gathered into Willy's pack. Tim returned to the room with the rope and tarp. Elaine opened the pack as Tim shoved his items in the pack on top of her supplies that she placed inside.

"Where's a good flashlight?" Willy asked.

"Here, this spotlight was in the equipment bag," Tim said and handed Willy the spotlight.

"Call Mark on the radio, and tell him I'm on the way to get them," Willy instructed Tim. "If he objects, tell him it's too late and that I'm already on my way. Tell Mark to be on the lookout for my spotlight, and when he sees it, shine his toward me or yell, or whatever it takes to get my attention, okay?"

Willy nodded toward the walkie-talkie radio and motioned for Tim to pick up the radio.

"Hey, Mark, do you read me?" Tim said.

Mark heard the radio. He had the radio lying on the top of his pack under the blanket that protected them from the rain.

"Yeah, Tim, got you loud and clear," Mark said slowly.

"Listen to me, Mark. Willy is on his way to get you and Andre. He's got some medicine for you, and we have come up with a makeshift splint for your leg. He's got the spotlight from the equipment bag. Do you think you can spot it coming down the road?"

"We're not far above the road," Mark said. "I'm sure I could spot a light coming down it, but I don't think it's a good idea—"

"Mark, too late," Tim interrupted. "Willy's on his way, so make sure to stay focused and watch for the light, okay?"

"Gotcha, I'll keep an eye out for him," Mark answered.

"Okay, he'll be there shortly," Tim replied.

"Roger that," Mark said.

Willy put on his rain jacket and zipped it up. He pulled the hood onto his head and secured it. He grabbed the backpack and placed it into position on his back. Willy slid the wooden legs through the straps of the pack and picked up the knife in one hand and the spotlight in the other. Willy looked at the others.

"Pray that I get to Mark in time and get back to the cabin with them," Willy said to the group.

Willy walked to the door. Everyone was silent. Willy opened the cabin door, walked out the door, and closed it. Willy never glanced at the second cabin. He made his way down the steps and up the path to the old, abandoned road. He turned left and battled the wind and rain as he hurried down the road. Right away, Willy noticed a musky odor filling the air.

\*\*\*

Mark sensed that something was with him and Andre in the forest. He sensed he was not alone. He still smelled the strong scent around them. He heard breaths from time to time over the sounds of the rain on the leaves and forest ground. He thought maybe there was hope with Willy coming. Mark unholstered the pistol as quietly as he could. He clicked off the safety. He held the gun tightly in his right hand and adjusted the emergency blanket so he could keep an eye out for Willy's spotlight. *If something bad happens,* Mark thought, *I'll fire the gun, and that would alert Willy to turn around.*

*\*\*\**

The game trail path that Ronnie and Shelley had taken to escape the shoreline and search for the old road was very slippery. They inched their way along the trail. It wasn't steep, but several tree roots zig zagged across it. The rain made the roots crossing the path dangerous, and if accidentally stepped on, one's footing could be lost in the blink of an eye.

Ronnie and Shelley experienced how difficult the trek had become. Each had fallen several times but progressed up the gentle slope. Shelley fell, and they stopped to regain their composure and get back to their feet. Whatever was shadowing them paused and patiently waited for them to start moving again. It continued up the slope beside them in the darkness of the forest. Ronnie barely lifted his feet as he shuffled them along on the ground. He slowly made his way forward, and Shelley provided light for him along the path.

The sounds that Shelley and Ronnie heard indicated that they were being followed. The creature's movements indicated that it was a very large animal, and the odor that surrounded them reminded them that it was near. They continued to trudge along like methodical machines. Both breathed hard like they had just finished a sprint race. Their heartbeats were at what seemed to be an impossible rate.

Ronnie started to ask Shelley to take a break when his right foot stepped on a tree root hidden under the leaves. The pressure of his step on the slippery roots caused Ronnie to fall. He crashed down on the path, falling on both knees. He slid frontwards and face planted into the mud. He held onto Stan's body the best he could.

Shelley turned and watched Ronnie gently move Stan's body. The body rested partially on Ronnie and partially in the leaves. The movement of whatever was following stopped. Shelley put one hand against a small tree and lowered herself to the ground. The wet ground and the continuous rainfall that never stopped did not bother them. Both of them were completely exhausted.

"I'm not sure I can get back on my feet, much less put Stan back on my shoulders," Ronnie confessed.

Shelley gasped for air and laid back into the leaves and closed her eyes.

"Ronnie, I can't make it any farther either," Shelley said between her gasps for air.

"Let's just rest a minute, Shelley," Ronnie said.

Shelley rolled onto her side and turned off the flashlight. She coughed several times in her effort to take in more air. Ronnie laid motionless. They heard a branch break.

They heard the rustling of the bushes, and they knew the creature moved toward them. Neither one of them had the capacity to do anything about it. They simply laid in their assumed positions and waited. Ronnie found Shelley's hand in the darkness and held it tightly. Shelley forced her eyes closed. She and Ronnie waited for the inevitable.

***

Tim and Elaine stared at the radio and waited on Mark to call and tell them that Willy had gotten to him and Andre. They hoped to hear that everything was okay.

Betty moved to the window. She had taken Willy's job of watching for Dave. Sasha stayed seated close to the fireplace.

Betty noticed that occasionally, she saw what appeared to be a small light shining on the porch floor and the deck railing at the front of the other cabin. The cup remained on the end table by the chair. Suddenly, something moved by the cup, but only for a second. She watched. It moved again. Betty realized the movement was the thin cloth place mat where the lamp sat. *What could move the mat without touching it? Maybe the wind?*

"Something's wrong," Betty said and focused on the front of the cabin.

"That's the understatement of the year, Betty," Sasha said sarcastically and lifted her head.

"I think the front door of the other cabin is open," Betty said. "I think the reason we ain't seen Dave is because he's not in the cabin." She wheeled around and looked at the others.

"Maybe he decided to join us over here," Sasha said.

"And not close the door?" Betty said. "Something's wrong, people."

Elaine moved to the window beside Betty and looked out. After a couple of seconds, she turned and faced Tim.

"I think she's right," Elaine said. "I can see the light on the deck, and the front door is open."

"Hey, he made his choices," Sasha said bitterly. "I'm not leaving this cabin if that's what you got in mind."

"I never said you had to do anything, Sasha," Elaine said forcefully. "I was just confirming what Betty said. In fact, I didn't say any of you had to do anything."

"Whoa, Elaine," Tim said calmly. "Let's not get too excited. The last thing we need to do is turn on each other."

"I'm not turning on anyone, Tim," Elaine said. "I just know that if I was out there in some kind of situation, I would like for someone to have the guts to come and help me."

"What are you going to do, Elaine?" Betty asked. "Go outside with... with whatever is out there?"

"I'm going to check on Dave," Elaine said.

"No way, Elaine. We all need to stay inside," Tim insisted.

"You people can sit on your rear ends if you want to!" Elaine exclaimed. "I came here as the medical personnel responsible for you people. If Dave needs assistance, it's my job to tend to him."

Elaine walked into the bedroom of the cabin. The others heard her moving things around in her mad search for what she deemed necessary to go next door and check on Dave. The three who remained in the front room of the cabin intermittently glanced at each other. At times, they made eye contact and shook their heads in disbelief. No one believed that Elaine was really going to do this.

It took Elaine several minutes to gather her supplies — tape, gauze, medicine, and the plastic bags for her supplies. Elaine placed everything she gathered into a small pack. She glanced around the room and tried to figure out if there was anything else she needed. Tim entered the room and stood in the doorway to watch Elaine.

"I'm concerned about your safety if you leave this cabin, Elaine," Tim said.

"My mind is made up, Tim," Elaine said. "I'm going to check on Dave. I appreciate your concern, and I understand the rationality of what others think. But if something is wrong with Dave, and I didn't go help, it would linger on my conscience. I've got to do this."

"So, if you are going out there in the darkness, I'll go with you, Elaine," Tim said bravely.

"No, Tim, this is my decision," Elaine replied. "It's something I've got to do. You stay here with Betty and Sasha. I think they're pretty creeped out, and it's hard to tell what they might do if we leave them alone in this cabin. I'll be alright. It'll only take a couple of minutes to run next door to assess the situation and get back here."

Elaine looked to her left and spotted the last thing on her list, which was a flashlight. She put on her jacket, put her pack on her back, and picked up the light. She moved toward the front of the cabin. Tim stepped aside and allowed her to move past him from the bedroom. Sasha and Betty looked up and watched Elaine. Tim followed Elaine.

"Elaine, I wish you would reconsider. Please don't go outside," Betty pleaded.

"It'll be okay, Betty," Elaine said. "I'll only be gone a couple of minutes. Just make sure you guys let me in when I get back, okay?"

"Okay, you got it," Betty said.

Elaine walked to the front door. Tim followed her. Elaine unlocked the door and the deadbolt. She turned to the others and switched on the flash-light.

"Wish me luck," Elaine said joyfully.

Tim patted Elaine on the shoulder.

"Hurry back," Tim said.

Elaine opened the door and headed for the steps. The cabin door shut. Elaine clearly heard the door's locks turning.

# CHAPTER 17

Willy tried to move as quickly as possible down the old road toward Mark. The footing was not as much a problem as the constant rain that beat against his face. He continuously switched the spotlight from one hand to the other so he could wipe the rainwater from his eyes. Willy could not believe the darkness that surrounded him. The beam of the light on the road split the darkness of the night. Every time he needed to clear his vision, Willy held the knife and the light in the same hand and was extra careful not to drop either.

He recalled how, back in Tennessee, one could go to some remote areas. Willy was used to the Nashville area. But just about everywhere you ventured out into the country, there would be a light that could be spotted somewhere in the distance. But here, there was nothing. Just darkness.

Willy continued to walk in the darkness. *Did I just hear something?* he thought. Willy paused. *What is that smell?* The odor moved down the road as Willy moved down the road. He knew there was something in the woods. Mark had told them he had seen it. No matter the pace Willy traveled, the damp, musky odor was around him all the time. Willy continued his pace and thought, *I hope I can reach Mark in time.*

Willy knew that Mark had a weapon. That was a much better option for safety than the knife he had taken from the drawer, but maybe there wasn't a good option. Willy thought, *Was the best option to wait for daylight to arrive and call Rob to come and pick me up? How far have I traveled? Have I already passed Mark? Is he still conscious? Will Mark even see my light? Come on, Mark, where are you?*

With Willy's next breath, he heard his name being called out. He stopped dead in his tracks. He searched the mountainside in front of him. He spotted the light that Mark waved back and forth. Willy signaled back and trekked up to Mark and Andre.

After several minutes of slipping, sliding, and pushing small bushes to the side that impeded his progress, Willy finally stood in front of Mark. He looked into Mark's eyes.

"You made it," Mark whispered.

Willy nodded and realized that he was looking at a broken man. But at least Mark was alert. Willy knelt down on his knees in front of Mark and removed the backpack. He took the tarp and covered them.

"I've got medicine," Willy explained. "And I got something to use for a splint for your leg."

"Willy, I don't think we are alone," Mark whispered. "I've been hearing things the entire time we have been sitting here."

"What kind of things, Mark?" Willy asked.

"Every now and then, I hear sounds like something taking a deep breath," Mark explained. "I don't think I'm imagining it, Willy. I've heard it too many times, and there is odor in the air."

"Yeah, I smell it, Mark," Willy said. "But I smelled it when I first left the cabin, and I smelled it all the way down the road. If the creature hasn't done anything yet, and I can't imagine why it hasn't, maybe it's not gonna do anything. Let's get this splint on, take some medicine, and get a move on."

"I'm not going to be able to walk, Willy, and I'm not leaving Andre," Mark said.

"I know, Mark. I'm going to drag you both on a tarp," Willy said.

"Are you sure?" Mark asked.

"I'll do the best I can," Willy said. "We'll just take our time and let the chips fall where they may."

Willy unfastened the bag with the medicine and retrieved a bottle of water from the pack. He carefully gave Mark just one dose of the pain pills and then the antibiotics. Mark took the medicine with the aid of about half of the contents of the water bottle. Willy took the water and downed the rest. Willy didn't know why, but he placed the empty water bottle back into the pack. He didn't want to litter the forest. He hated to see trash lying around anywhere. He tried to do his part in keeping the land clean.

He slowly fitted Mark with the makeshift splint and secured it in place. Mark winced a couple of times, but both knew it was a necessary pain he had to endure. Willy took the tarp that was covering them and spread it out on the ground. He carefully positioned Mark and Andre on it.

"Hang in there," Willy said, and they started down the mountain.

They had gone only about ten feet when Willy stopped to adjust his handhold on the tarp. Both men heard the low grunt, then the sound of something moving through the forest. Mark positioned and pointed the gun to fire out into the darkness. Willy stood frozen in his tracks. The men realized the movement in the trees was moving away from their location. There had definitely been something watching them, but it was leaving. *Why did it just leave?* Mark thought. He relaxed his arm and switched the safety of the gun back to the safe position. He rested the pistol back on his chest.

Willy slowly regained his composure and gently pulled the tarp again. The only grunt sounds now were coming from Mark as the sharp pains would periodically shoot through his lower leg. Even though they were going downhill, it took some time to reach the road. With one final tug, all three were on the road and headed back to the cabins.

\*\*\*

Elaine loosened her grip on the handrail as she moved down the steps. She made her way to the contestants' cabin. Immediately, she noticed that the front door was open. *They were correct*, she thought.

The odor filled the air and was stifling to Elaine. She climbed the steps to the deck of the other cabin, and she scanned the wooden planks of the deck with her flashlight. There was nothing to see but the puddles of water and the raindrops impacting them as they fell. She slowly placed one foot in front of the other as she made her way to the opened door. She found it eerily interesting how the wind moved the door back and forth and provided a small light to the deck flooring, only to take it away.

As Elaine touched the door, she briefly thought of how the scene reminded her of the many scary moments in movies that she had watched. She paused and looked into the front room of the cabin. She entered the cabin, but nothing seemed to be out of place. The coffee mug sat on the small table. The fire gently popped, and the wood crackled and continued to burn slowly. The only odd thing about the room was the quietness.

Elaine moved to the chair that Dave was relaxing in. She peered around the room and called for Dave and waited for a response. There was no response. She called out a second time, but still there was no answer. Elaine searched the cabin and was unsure of what she might find.

\*\*\*

"Elaine's in the cabin," Betty announced to the others as she saw Elaine step beyond the end table that the coffee cup sat on.

"Do you see Dave?" Tim asked and stared simultaneously at the pistol and the radio.

"No, just Elaine," Betty said. "She's moving through the cabin...heading for the bedroom."

"Try to keep an eye on her and make sure she's okay," Tim said.

The light in the bedroom of the cabin next door came on. Betty could see Elaine enter the room.

"She's in the bedroom now, just standing in the middle of it and looking around," Betty detailed.

"Just keep watching her, Betty. Keep her in your sight if you can," Tim repeated.

There was a small flash of lightning somewhere near the opening of the bay and the rumble of thunder in the distance. Betty flinched and jumped back from the window. "Sorry, people! That kind of caught me off guard."

"That's all we need," Sasha said. "Add a little thunder and lightning to the moment. My nerves are already shot, guys."

\*\*\*

Elaine also jumped when the flash of lightning swept through the room. She thought, *Where's Dave? He's obviously not in the cabin, and he didn't come over to us.*

Elaine turned and walked back into the front room of the cabin, and there was nothing out of place. There was an empty mug and the empty chair. As Elaine walked to the front door, Betty continued to give the others a blow-by-blow account of Elaine's every move. Each time Elaine stopped and looked throughout a room, Betty informed them of her exact actions.

When Elaine got to the door, she switched the flashlight back on and walked onto the deck outside. She shut the door.

"Dave, where are you?" Elaine wondered aloud.

Elaine decided Dave had to be there somewhere. She rounded the corner and faced the crew cabin. She made her way down that side of the cabin. She continued to scan the deck and the bushes and look for any sign of Dave. Elaine would pinch her nostrils together and hoped that this might alleviate the musky odor around her.

Betty watched Elaine's every step as she searched outside. Betty told the others about her every movement. Betty couldn't believe Elaine was brave enough to be out there alone.

Tim stared intently at radio, but now he was also thinking about Elaine. He thought, *What if something bad happened? What kind of a man am I to let her go out there alone? I did try to convince her not to go in the first place.*

Elaine turned and walked back to the front of the cabin. She started to go down the steps and paused. *There's another side to the cabin*, she thought. She stood there and pondered whether she wanted to venture around the corner out of Betty's sight. Elaine had never made direct eye contact with Betty, but she glanced a few times to make sure that Betty was still watching. This time, Elaine looked directly at her and moved to the hidden side of the cabin.

"Where are you going, Elaine?" Betty said. "Don't...I can't see you, girl. Don't go around that corner."

"What is she doing, Betty?" Sasha asked.

"She's going around the other side of the cabin," Betty said. "I can't see her now." She faced Sasha.

Elaine shook so badly that she could barely focus the flashlight. She scanned the light around the railing and to the back corner of the cabin. In the outer edges of the light, she spotted an object. Elaine moved the main beam of the light to it, and right away, she recognized it to be a human arm.

It was attached to nothing. It was just lying on the wooden plank that met the cabin wall. Elaine gasped loudly. She stared at the arm for a few seconds, and a sudden rush of fear ran through her entire body. The walk to the severed arm was a short distance, but her steps to it seemed to take forever. Elaine knelt on one knee and removed the pack. She brought nothing that she could use to wrap the arm, so she removed her jacket and folded it around it. *Poor Dave*, she thought.

"We need to check on her," Betty informed Tim. "She's been around that side too long."

"Hey, she said it was something she had to do," Sasha reminded everyone. "We never said we would go look for her if she didn't come back."

"Betty, Sasha's right," Tim said coldly. "Elaine should have never left the cabin, and as selfish as it sounds, Mark told us to stay put. What Willy and Elaine have done was their own choice."

Betty clearly showed a look of disgust. Fear was on her face as she turned and looked out the window. There was a bright flash from the lightning as the bolt slammed into the middle of the bay. The thunder's roar shook the walls of the cabin. Elaine crouched down as the shock waves of the thunder impacted her body. She quickly came to her feet and held the backpack and flashlight in one hand and gripped the severed arm with the other. She made her way to the front of the cabin and stayed close to the cabin wall. She decided that when she got to the steps, she would choose the right moment and make a mad dash for the other cabin.

The bright flash of the lightning gave Betty a split second to see what was on the opposite side of the glass at the window. A hand and arm came crashing through the glass. Sasha screamed as the creature wrapped its fingers around Betty's neck. It ripped her through the opened window where the glass had been.

Tim, in one quick motion, grabbed the gun and fired a round in the direction of where Betty stood. The bullet struck the trim around the window and sent little splinters of wood flying through the air.

Outside, Betty was tossed around like a ragdoll. Her feet, legs, and arms all impacted the side of the cabin and the railing around the deck. The sickening thumps against the wood of the cabin could clearly be heard by Sasha and Tim. The creature made sure there was no more life in Betty's body.

The Hairy Man held Betty's limp, broken body at arm's length. Her neck was just barely attached to the rest of her body. She was covered in blood. There was a trickle of blood that ran down the creature's hand. It slowly dripped onto the deck. It was satisfied that Betty was dead. It wheeled around and launched her body high into the air toward the bay. The creature leaned back and raised its arms, letting out a high-pitched yell that almost sounded like a scream.

Elaine did not hear the glass break, but she definitely heard the gunshot and the scream. She stopped and leaned against the corner of the cabin. She slowly slid down the wall until her legs folded and she sat on her bottom. Elaine was afraid to even peek around the corner, much less move in that direction. She sat silently in that position and tried to figure out what she should do.

# CHAPTER 18

Tim stood beside the table and waved the pistol in every direction, trying to predict the creature's next move. Sasha stood in front of the fireplace and was frozen by fear. She stared at Tim. They could not grasp what had just taken place. Without warning, the glass in the bedroom window shattered into a million pieces.

Tim wheeled around immediately and squeezed off a shot aimlessly through the bedroom door. He believed that he saw something move across the doorway. At first, he concluded that he had seen something, but now he wasn't sure. Tim knew he couldn't waste ammo on ghosts or things he thought he'd seen. Silently, he positioned himself in the middle of the room, so that if anything rushed them, he might be able to react in time.

A large rock as big as a softball was hurled through the broken window in the direction of Sasha. It careened off the top of the sofa and slammed in front of the fireplace. Sasha jumped to the left to avoid the rock and moved toward Tim. She passed the end of the fireplace, and suddenly, there was a loud thud. The front door was kicked completely off its hinges to the inside of the cabin.

The corner of the door struck Sasha directly at the back of her neck, driving her face down to the cabin floor. Tim turned and, without aiming, fired the pistol. There was nothing on the deck outside, only the darkness of the night. Tim was sure he heard movement on the wooden planks of the deck. He was sure that, from time to time, something darted by the windows. Each time Tim caught a glimpse of something or imagined he saw something, he fired the gun. He rotated his position and looked for the next direction of an attack.

Then everything got quiet. *It's too quiet*, Tim thought. He moved and looked through the bedroom door. It stood looking directly back at Tim through the doorway.

*This dark, hairy figure is poised just like a man*, Tim thought. Tim froze for a couple of seconds. He slowly raised the pistol to take aim but stopped about halfway through the motion. *How can I shoot something that looks so human, something that looks like somebody?* Tim studied the creature in awe. It stared back at him.

Tim thought in a panic, *Why isn't it moving toward me? Why isn't it attacking?* The answers came all too quickly as Tim heard the cabin floor creak behind him. Two massive arms wrapped around Tim's chest and squeezed. He pulled the trigger one last time, but the shot was aimless. Tim merely squeezed the trigger hard enough to fire a shot before his body gave way to the immense pressure. Tim felt a heated rush run through his brain as his sternum crushed. The splintered bone fragments penetrated his internal organs. All went dark. Tim was dead.

Sasha regained consciousness and used her hands to push herself up onto her knees. The high-pitched scream from behind the creature caused it to drop Tim's body to the floor. It swung around. Sasha's hands clutched the sides of her head just as the advertisements for old horror movies depicted on posters at the theater.

She screamed until the creature's foot drove deep into Sasha's chest. The sudden impact knocked her halfway through the opening, where the door once stood. The back of her head violently slammed into the deck floor. Another hand grabbed Sasha by her hair and dragged her outside.

She barely realized what was taking place.

The blow to the chest damaged her aorta, and life was quickly fleeing Sasha. By the time the creature emerged through the door opening, Sasha was gone.

The two figures on the deck began to grunt and stomped on Sasha's body until she was barely recognizable. One of them grabbed her and hurled Sasha into the bushes beside the cabin.

\*\*\*

The mysterious sounds of something drew closer to Ronnie and Shelley. The sounds were getting louder. They heard bushes being pushed aside, and the water accumulated on them could be heard falling to the ground. Ronnie knew it was very close. He gave Shelley's hand a little extra squeeze.

The sound stopped. Shelley sensed that whatever had been following them was now standing beside them. Ronnie and Shelley waited for whatever was going to happen. Neither one of them dared to even try to raise their heads and look. The creature crouched down in the darkness and slowly observed the pair as they laid on the wet ground and gasped for air. Shelley could not only smell but feel its breath faintly move her hair each time it exhaled. *What's it waiting for?* she thought.

Shelley felt something slide underneath her elbow and gently raise her arm off the ground. She realized it was the fingers of the creature as it gripped her. Shelley wanted to scream, but she didn't have it in her anymore.

Shelley was lifted to an almost standing position. She felt another arm press against the back of her legs at the knees. The creature carried Shelley. It cradled her much like someone carrying a small child up the mountainside. Shelley became overtaken with so much fear and exhaustion, she simply passed out. She never felt the wet bushes rubbing against her boots or her head as the creature carried her up the hill.

Ronnie tried to reason as to why the creature took Shelley away. He thought, *Why didn't it just finish her off at that spot? Did it think I was dead too?*

The noises coming down the hill told Ronnie all he needed to know. It was coming for him. Ronnie thought of his family and how he was never going to see them again. He knew it was getting close. He wondered, *Will my wife ever really know what happened to me? Will there be closure for her and the kids?*

Ronnie felt the creature move Stan's body to the side. He felt the massive hand and arm slide through the mud underneath his midsection. Ronnie heard something else going on in the wet leaves but wasn't totally sure what it was. Ronnie realized the creature was picking up Stan's body. Both Ronnie and Stan's body were lifted off the ground.

The creature moved up the mountainside. Ronnie felt the animal taking enormous strides with ease as they made their way through the forest. The creature was huge and could do anything it wanted to do with them. Ronnie was confused as to why had the creature waited so long to make contact. The creature knew it was in control, and this was its home and territory.

Abruptly, the movement stopped. Ronnie was hanging in midair. He sensed they were on flat ground. It was the old roadbed below him. The creature knelt and carefully placed Ronnie on the ground. Ronnie's arm bumped against Shelley's backpack. He felt Stan's body come to rest against his back. Ronnie had no idea what was taking place, and he tried to imagine what was going through the creature's mind.

*Why had it placed them there? And where were they heading?* Ronnie fought to remain conscious, even though Ronnie wasn't sure why he should. However, eventually, his body gave in to all that had transpired, and he drifted into a world of darkness.

***

Willy pulled the tarp a few feet behind him and turned around. He tugged it with his body and moved it backwards up the road. It was only a few feet of progress at a time. Willy stopped to rest. Mark was doing his best to fight off the pain in his ankle.

Willy dropped to his knees to rest.

"Willy, cover me and Andre with the tarp and go back to the cabin," Mark said. "When daylight breaks, you can bring some help back with you."

Willy believed he heard a gunshot in the distance. The bright flash of the lightning and the deafening thunder made him almost jump out of his hiking boots. He believed he heard a couple more shots fired, but he wasn't sure. The wind and rain made hearing anything nearly impossible. He knew that they were still a pretty good way from the cabins. Willy assumed that Mark did not hear the shots, or he would have said something. But he knew, too, that the pain medicine had kicked in, and Mark wasn't sure of a lot of things.

"No way, buddy," Willy replied. "We're in this together now. I was scared to death coming down this road by myself in the dark, and I'm definitely not going back up it by myself."

Both men chuckled.

"Plus, you got the gun, and I'm not leaving the gun either," Willy added.

This time, the men laughed.

"I'm not too sure the gun would do a person any good," Mark said. "I'm telling you, Willy, I've never seen anything like that thing up on the side of the mountain. That thing was huge, Willy. It looked like a gigantic man covered with hair...it was huge."

"I don't get it, Mark," Willy said. "Why did it attack you and Andre coming off the mountain and then just sit there and watch you guys until I got there? That doesn't make any sense. And then, for it to just walk off as soon as we started down the mountain? It doesn't make sense."

"I don't know, Willy. But I'm telling you, I've never been as scared as I was sitting on that mountainside in the dark. I could hear it breathe — long, deep breaths. It was almost like it wanted me to know it was there or something."

Willy slowly came to his feet and once again gripped the tarp tightly with his hands.

"Let's go a little further, Mark," Willy said.

Mark laid flat on his back and rested the pistol on his chest. The tarp slid in the dirt of the old road. Willy pulled it about ten feet at a time. He rested for a minute and then repeated the process. Oddly enough, Willy noticed the rain started to subside somewhat. The raindrops no longer pounded his face and dripped off his chin.

The pain medicine was now doing its job on Mark. He would drift off, then bounce back to reality. But soon, Mark faded off to sleep and no longer felt the pain in his ankle. Suddenly, Willy's footing slipped, and he fell face first into the mud of the old road.

He didn't have time to turn loose of the tarp to use his hands to break his fall. He wasn't sure if he could get back to his feet, much less pull the tarp. He laid on the ground. He heard something rustling the small trees. It was coming down the bank just ahead of them. He heard the footsteps in the soaked soil of the road. Willy knew he didn't have any fight left in him. He laid there face down in the mud and waited.

He felt the pack move slightly on his back. He realized that whatever was touching the pack was gripping a large portion of the material to hold onto. To Willy's surprise, he was partially lifted off the road. He heard the funny sound a tarp makes when someone is trying to work the wrinkles out of it. Willy laid quiet. He heard the tarp slide on the road. He felt the toes of his boots drag through in the mud as they moved and headed up the road.

*Where is it taking us?* Willy thought.

\*\*\*

Elaine sat on the outside the deck and hugged the side of the cabin. The night around the cabins became silent. She trembled with fear. She was afraid to move. She thought, *Do I dare return to the crew's cabin? Should I go to the cabin? Is the door locked? Maybe I should hide till someone can help. Does someone next door need help? I have to find a way to check on the others.*

Elaine finally got the courage to move. She tilted her head forward and peeked around the corner. She watched for several seconds, and there was no movement she could see anywhere. Elaine slowly rolled up onto her knees and came to a standing position. Cautiously, she walked to the steps and slid her hand down the rail. Her boots made contact with the trail that led to the crew's cabin. She switched on the flashlight and controlled her footsteps between the cabins. Her hands shook uncontrollably. She heard her heart pound in her chest. Elaine wasn't sure what was driving her. Was it fear or the adrenalin of the moment? She knew that it was probably both.

When she arrived at the front of the other cabin, Elaine walked the steps one at a time. She planted one foot solidly on the wooden step before she lifted the other foot. As the flashlight shined on the deck flooring between the steps and the door, Elaine saw the ruby red blood splattered on the planks. She scanned the deck and looked for the source of the blood. There was nothing that indicated where the blood came from.

She looked through the door and saw Tim lying motionless on the floor at the end of the counter. *Whose blood was on the deck?* she thought.

She saw the blood trickling out of the corner of Tim's mouth. Elaine took a brief moment and studied Tim to see if there was any movement to indicate that he might be breathing. There was none.

Elaine made her way to the bedroom to see if anyone might be hiding there. She noticed a small, bright red drop on the floor as she entered the room. She looked around and saw the creature squatted down beside one of the bunks, like a frightened child. She gasped.

She and the creature made eye contact, and the creature dropped its head and stared at the floor. Elaine noticed that it was injured. It was scared. Elaine didn't understand why, but she knew she had to help the creature, even though its own kind had killed her friends. She thought, *I might as well help someone and do some good. After all, that's what I was brought here to do.*

Elaine was surprised to realize that she had referred to the creature as *someone.* That was odd. But the creature appeared to be almost human in nature. She soon realized that the creature was a juvenile and truly frightened.

Elaine slowly lowered herself to the floor and scooted in its direction. The creature glanced at Elaine and immediately dropped its eyes back to the floor. It seemed to have a certain amount of trust in Elaine and her movements.

Once beside the creature, Elaine gently placed her hand on the back of the creature's hand and brushed it ever so easily. Once trust was established, she lifted the creature's hand away from the wound. It was only a small, shallow wound across the bicep, but it needed attention. Elaine was sure there would be no problem in taking care of this one. Slowly, Elaine opened the bag she had taken with her to the other cabin. She removed the supplies. The creature watched her actions intently. It showed trust in her. Elaine hoped it would continue to be calm as she administered the first aid. She softly spoke to the creature as she cleaned the wound.

"This will help you," Elaine whispered.

The creature sat there calmly as she dabbed the antiseptic. The shallow wound stopped bleeding by the time Elaine applied the triple antibiotic. She lowered the tube and pushed herself back from the juvenile. To Elaine's surprise, the juvenile raised its hand and extended its fingers toward her. She set the tube of medicine in her lap and raised her own hand. Elaine placed the palm of her hand underneath the hand of the young creature. She smiled, and for a moment, they stared into each other's eyes.

The creature turned its head and looked toward the door of the bedroom. Elaine realized they were not alone. She had concentrated so intently on what she was doing that she never heard the other one enter the room. Elaine turned and looked as the juvenile stood and approached the other creature. Elaine assumed it was the smaller creature's mother. The mother took the hand of the young juvenile and approached Elaine.

The smaller one was probably a little over four feet tall, and the mother was at least seven feet tall. They stopped within a couple steps of Elaine. She heard her heart pound inside her chest. She tried not to show her fear. The large creature extended its arm toward Elaine. She returned the gesture just like she had done earlier with the child creature. The mother creature placed a smooth, round stone into the palm of Elaine's hand.

Elaine closed her fingers and tightly gripped the warm rock. The two creatures turned and made their way out of the cabin, going through the bedroom door. The younger one turned and looked at Elaine one last time. Elaine raised her hand and waved back to it. Within a few short seconds, the creatures made their way through the front room. They went out of the door and into the darkness, and they were gone. The night fell silent, and even the rain stopped and no longer hit the roof of the cabin.

Elaine never got up from the bedroom floor. She pulled a sleeping bag off one of the bunks and unzipped it. She covered herself with the sleeping bag and leaned back against the wall. Elaine held the stone tightly in her hand. She knew it had meaning and had been given to her for a reason. *What is the reason? I have no idea.* Elaine sat there and pondered over all that had taken place. The warmth of the sleeping bag took effect, and she faded off into dreamland.

# CHAPTER 19

When Ronnie woke up, he wasn't sure if he was dreaming or actually awake. He heard the birds chirping and the flutter of their wings as they darted from one tree limb to another. The sounds surrounded him and were peaceful as he laid there listening. He recalled the events of the day and night before. *How could things be so serene now?* he thought.

Ronnie felt the warmth against his face, even though the dampness still filled the air. He cautiously opened his eyes. He was met with the morning sun shining directly on his face. Ronnie rolled onto his back and observed a makeshift tent covering them. He knew he wasn't dreaming because Shelley and Stan's body were under the shelter with him.

Ronnie gently placed his hand on Shelley's shoulder. He nudged her. There was no response. He touched her again, and on the second shake, she jerked. She immediately raised and sat up. Shelley turned and looked at Ronnie.

She gasped loudly and sucked in the morning air. Both noticed the air was crispy, fresh, and void of any musky fragrance or odor.

"I think it's okay, Shelley," Ronnie said. "Slide out the opening." He nudged Shelley on the shoulder.

At first, Shelley was reluctant to do so, but eventually she scooted on her bottom out of the opening of the shelter that covered them. Ronnie grabbed

ahold of Stan's body and slowly exited through the opening, crawling backwards and pulling Stan's body. Once outside, they both studied the shelter
in amazement. They had been placed on the upper side of the road. There
were tree limbs about the size of a person's arm that laid from the top of the
bank down to the road and covered them. Limbs from small pine trees were
set on top of the tree limbs to protect the three of them from the elements.
It was a crude but efficient shelter.

"Ronnie, did you make this?" Shelley asked.

"No," Ronnie answered. "The last thing I remember is being laid on the
road."

"Why...why are we still alive?" Shelley asked slowly.

"I have no idea," Ronnie said. "All I know is that we are. There's no
rhyme or reason for this. Let's try to make it to the cabins."

Ronnie bent down on one knee and gripped Stan's wrist, slid the other
arm between Stan's legs, and with the help of Shelley, he hoisted Stan's
body across his shoulders and rose to his feet. He adjusted Stan's body and
took one more look at the shelter before they began to move down the road.

They had been placed at the edge of the forest, where it met the clearing
that contained the cabins. The warmth of the morning sun was a welcome
feeling as they journeyed between the small bushes that bordered the road.
Neither of them talked, not even when the tops of the cabins came into
view. They continued to just put one foot in front of the other as they made
their way to the cabins.

\*\*\*

Willy awoke and slowly opened his eyes. He took in the majestic view
of the bay from the cabin deck. He turned and looked at Mark. Mark was
already awake and looking out over the water.

"Morning there, sleeping beauty," Mark said and made eye contact with

Willy. "How was your night?"

"Just peachy. Yours?" Willy said and smiled.

"Thanks for coming for us, man," Mark said. "Thanks for dragging us back to the cabins. I don't know how you pulled it off." He turned back and looked toward the bay,

"I only brought you and Andre part of the way, Mark," Willy confessed. "I collapsed on the road as I was pulling you guys. Something else dragged all three of us here. It apparently laid us on the deck." Willy leaned his head against the outside of the cabin.

"What did you see?" Mark asked.

"Nothing really," Willy said. "I remember something grabbing my back-pack...I remember hearing the crackling noise of the tarp...and I remember the toes of my boots dragging in the mud."

"You honestly didn't drag us here?" Mark asked.

"No, Mark. I tried. Something else brought us back here."

Willy turned and looked out over the bay. He heard someone call out his name. It was Shelley. Shelley and Ronnie were walking down the path that connected the old, abandoned road to the cabins. Willy made his way to them and helped with Stan.

They all made their way up to the deck of the cabin. Willy placed Stan's body next to Andre. He took a long look at the spot where the cabin's door had stood. He walked up the opening and looked inside. Willy noticed Tim lying motionless on the floor next to the counter. He wondered, *What else is in here?*

"Is there anyone in here?" Willy shouted.

Elaine removed the sleeping bag from around her neck. She heard peo-ple talking. Elaine jumped to her feet and ran to the bedroom door. There stood Willy. She sprinted to the front of the cabin and wrapped her arms around Willy. Tears flowed down her face.

"Where are the others?" Willy asked softly.

"It's just me. There are no others," Elaine said calmly and wiped the tears from her cheek.

"Are you sure, Elaine?" Shelley asked in disbelief.

Elaine looked at Shelley and started to answer, but hesitated when she noticed four rocks that had been placed on the railing of the crew's cabin. Elaine walked past Willy. There were no stones lying on the railing of the contestants' cabin. The others watched Elaine and waited for her response. She turned and faced them.

"Oh, I'm sure," Elaine said. "There's a stone for each of us." She pointed to the rocks on the railing.

All four looked at the four stones and back to Elaine.

"There are four rocks, Elaine, but five of us," Willy said.

Elaine slid her hand into the pocket of her Khaki pants. She removed the rock. She positioned the rock in her hand with her palm up, which was in the same manner she had received it. She extended her closed hand and loosened the grip on the stone. She slowly opened her fingers, exposing the smooth rock she held.

"Mine was given to me personally," Elaine said as her voice trembled.

The four others stared at Elaine, speechless. She shared her story and described all that had taken place the night before. No one interrupted her, and she had their full attention. Elaine detailed everything she knew and described from the time Willy left the cabin to the moment she received the rock. She explained how the creatures left her. Elaine finished her story.

All studied the stone in her hand when the SAT Phone came to life with a loud ring. Ronnie hurried into the cabin, located the phone, and pressed the answer button.

"Come get us as soon as possible," Ronnie said with a sense of urgency.

Rob tried to ask questions, but Ronnie interrupted.

"Bring the boat, now!" Ronnie demanded. "Mark has a broken ankle, and there are only five survivors left at the cabins. We need to leave!"

Ronnie ended the call.

The captain immediately picked up the phone inside the command center and called the dock where the boat was located. The captain informed the crew to ready the vessel and plan to depart as soon as he arrived. Within fifteen minutes, the captain, crew, and Rob were on their way back to the port to pick up the survivors and the deceased individuals at the cabins.

"Why us?" Shelley asked. "Why are we still alive?"

"I have a theory," Elaine answered. "I believe the ones still alive tried to help someone else. I know it sounds stupid, but think about it a minute."

"What are you talking about, Elaine?" Ronnie asked.

"As crazy as it sounds, think about it," Elaine said. "Ronnie and Shelley never left Stan. Mark never left Andre. Willy went to rescue Mark and Andre. I went to look for Dave, and I helped the young creature."

"Are you telling me that because we showed compassion for others, these creatures did the same for us?" Shelley asked.

"That does kind of make sense," Mark said. "It attacked Andre and me after we left Mr. Long lying in the forest. But it just sat with me as I held Andre. It was almost like it was guarding us. And as Willy began to drag us off the mountain, the creature just walked away. It could have done anything it wanted at any time."

"We know that there are several creatures here, people," Shelley said. "We all were having contact with them at the same time. That would mean that, socially, they may be more like humans than any of us thought. You're saying that they can reason quite effectively." Shelley looked out over the bay.

"I think they can reason quite well, and they may just work together better than any common group of people we know," Elaine said.

"You know, most people don't believe what the inhabitants of the fishing village told them over seventy years ago," Ronnie said. "They're probably not gonna believe this story either." He sounded disappointed.

"I say we let Rob and the networks take care of it. I just want to go home," Shelley said.

The steady hum of the boat engine entering the bay was a welcome sound to each and every one of them. Soon, everyone, including the deceased individuals at the cabin, were safely on the boat. They headed out of the bay.

Elaine was the only one who stood on the deck of the boat. She was wrapped in a blanket and sipped on a cup of hot chocolate. The boat passed a small opening along the shore, and she spotted the mother and the younger creature standing on a large rock.

Elaine stretched out her hand, and the juvenile mimicked the gesture. Suddenly, the two of them disappeared into the dark forest. Elaine took another sip and turned to go inside. The only person who witnessed what just happened was the captain. He nodded and smiled at Elaine as she entered the warm room of the boat.

Elaine took a seat and got comfortable for the boat ride back.

# ACKNOWLEDGMENTS

I would like to thank my wife, Tammy, for reading each chapter of the book for its content. Her encouragement inspired me to continue writing page after page.

## Don't Miss the Next Book!

On the one year anniversary of the events that took place at the abandoned fishing village, another expedition has been organized to return to Port Chatham. Not everyone in the search party is fully aware of just what awaits them at the port; only a few know for sure.

www.ingramcontent.com/pod-product-compliance
Lightning Source LLC
Chambersburg PA
CBHW060646260626
47161CB00008B/3025